Advance praise for
LAST OF THE NAME

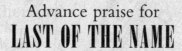

"*Last of the Name* is a rich, brave, brawling novel of the immigrant experience, bringing the cacophony of Civil War-era New York City vividly to life. Painstakingly researched, this story of holding on to family and heritage while making a new home in America is told with poetry, humor, and heart."

—Susan Fletcher, author of *Shadow Spinner*,
Walk Across the Sea, and *Journey of the Pale Bear*

"With loving attention to detail, Rosanne Parry recreates Civil War-era New York City and the struggles of intrepid Irish immigrants. More than a survival story, *Last of the Name* is a celebration of the power of music and family to sustain us through hard times. Truly a grand adventure!"

—Deborah Hopkinson, author of
How I Became a Spy: A Mystery of WWII London

"Civil War New York springs to life with danger, humor, and grit. You can feel the dance steps as a young immigrant's family traditions bring him strength and connection in a challenging new world. Historical fiction with a strong resonance today."

—Emily Whitman, author of *The Turning*

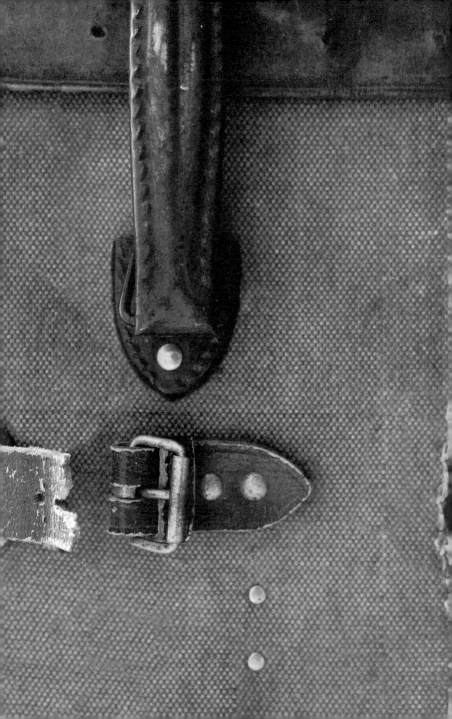

LAST

OF

THE

NAME

ROSANNE PARRY

CAROLRHODA BOOKS
MINNEAPOLIS

Carolrhoda Books
A division of Lerner Publishing Group, Inc.
241 First Avenue North
Minneapolis, MN 55401 USA

For reading levels and more information, look up this title at
www.lernerbooks.com.

Image credits: natsa/Shutterstock.com (waves); Regina Bilan/Shutterstock.com (ship); Daniel Balogh/EyeEm/Getty Images (suitcase); The British Library (Ireland map); THEPALMER/Getty Images (New York map); Social Media Hub/Shutterstock.com (line pattern); Ratana21/Shutterstock.com (paper). Map © Laura Westlund/Independent Picture Service.

Main body text set in Bembo Std 12.5/17.
Typeface provided by Monotype Typography.

Library of Congress Cataloging-in-Publication Data

Names: Parry, Rosanne, author.
Title: Last of the name / by Rosanne Parry.
Description: Minneapolis : Carolrhoda Books, [2019] | Summary: 1863, twelve-year-old Danny and his older sister Kathleen arrive in New York City to start a new life, but they soon find themselves navigating new prejudices and struggles.
Identifiers: LCCN 2018015861 (print) | LCCN 2018024280 (ebook) | ISBN 9781541542358 (eb pdf) | ISBN 9781541541597 (th : alk. paper)
Subjects: | CYAC: Irish Americans—Fiction. | Immigrants—Fiction. | Brothers and sisters—Fiction. | New York (N.Y.)—History—1775–1865—Fiction. | United States—History—Civil War, 1861-1865—Fiction.
Classification: LCC PZ7.P248 (ebook) | LCC PZ7.P248 Las 2019 (print) | DDC [Fic]—dc23

LC record available at https://lccn.loc.gov/2018015861

Manufactured in the United States of America
1-45333-38983-11/15/2018

FOR BRIAN,
AND ALL THE DANCERS BEFORE HIM
WHO KEPT THE TRADITION ALIVE.

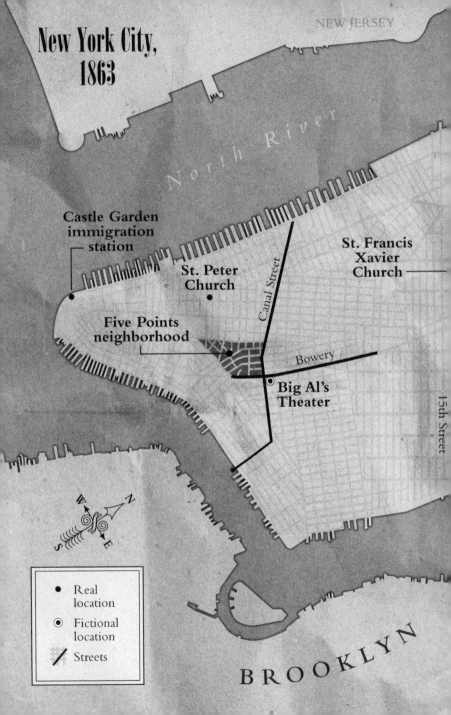

New York City, 1863

NEW JERSEY

North River

Castle Garden
immigration
— station

St. Peter
Church

St. Francis
Xavier
Church —

Canal Street

Five Points
neighborhood

Bowery

Big Al's
Theater

15th Street

W N
S E

BROOKLYN

●	Real location
⊙	Fictional location
▦ ╱	Streets

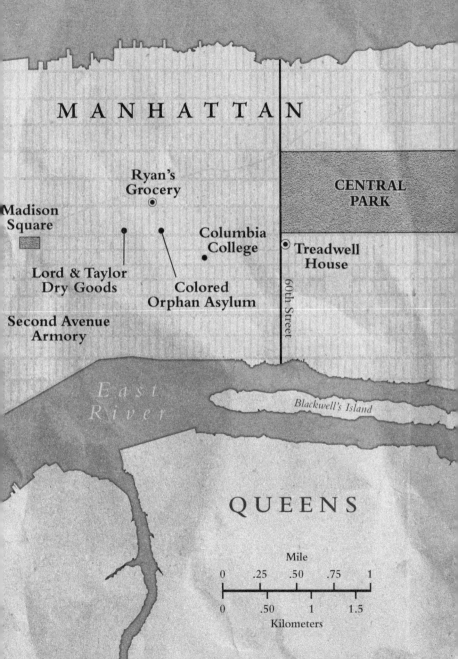

CHAPTER 1

THURSDAY, MARCH 19, 1863

Granny says I'm seven devils in one pair of shoes. She doesn't know the half of it. Trouble is always nipping at my heels.

Tonight it's me and all seven of them devils, tiptoeing past sleeping folk in the hold, and them that are coughing too hard to sleep. I step over bags and babies. I skirt around foul-smelling puddles and kick at rats. I can't just lie in the dark and hear Granny cough and feel her shaking with fever and do nothing. If Kathleen gives up her daily bread for me one more time I'll die of shame. If I was bigger I'd clout her over the head and make her eat her own portion fair and square. She was having none of it.

"You're the last of the name, Daniel O'Carolan," she said to me over the midday ration. "I swore I'd protect you and you'll eat what I give you or take a hiding that'll flay the skin right off you."

Granny won't take her food either. Our whole long walk from the poorhouse in Ballyvourney to the docks in Cove, she divided out every crumb we ever begged for in three even shares. But the fever has hold of her by the throat and she's changed.

"All the strength goes to you now," she said to me. She handed back the bread. "You two will need every bit of it."

"You'll eat what I give you," Kathleen said to Granny, sliding straight into the role of woman of the house without invitation. "It's you we need," she added. "We don't know a soul in New York."

"You'll not be alone," Granny said.

She tapped her bundle with a knowing smile. She's kept it at her side ever since last summer, when the landlord burned us out of our home. She's guarded it fiercely day and night. When I ask her what's in it, she only says, "It's ours" and tells wild stories about the old kings of Ireland and their great feasts in their golden halls and the master harpers who sang and played for the dancing. The more feverish she gets, the more she slips into this shadow world where the Irish are the kings. Where you can sing the old songs and dance the jigs and reels without fear of prison. She tells her wild tales over and again until she's worn out.

"Do something!" I said to Kathleen.

If it were a wound, she'd have her needle and thread out like a shot. There's nothing she can't mend in the way of cloth. Stitched the brothers back together more than once, she has.

"There's nothing to do but pray," she said

She counted out the rosary on a knotted string. I said my prayers already, counted them out on my fingers ten times over. Maybe God can't hear me for the coughing.

I can't bear it a moment longer. I won't. Granny needs food. Real food. I find the galley steps in the dark and tiptoe onto the deck.

After the hold, fresh air is as sweet as clean water. I creep across the deck in darkness. The crew eats better than us. If I could get to their stores, Granny would get stronger. She's had nothing but moldy bread and shriveled potatoes. I tiptoe along the rail to the galley door. Not a sound comes from inside.

The food is in the brig, under lock and chain. The shadows in the passageway give me cover. A single lamp swings above. Casks and chests are stacked shoulder high. I run to the brig, turn sideways, breathe all the way out, and slide through the bars. My shirt tears, and a bit of my skin, but I'm inside!

The smell of food—a whole roomful—it almost brings me to my knees. More food in this one spot than I've seen in a lifetime. For a moment, I take a notion of cracking open the barrels and feasting like a lord. But I know better. I only need a little. Something to bring a dash of color to Granny's face. A morsel of anything that will give her the strength to stand.

I duck down and worm my way through the barrels. A musty smell betrays which ones hold the rations they've been feeding the passengers. Smaller casks of rum and salt beef and smoked fish are off to one side. I can only dream of such rich fare. Granny'd never be able to eat them, sick as she is. There's a rime of mold on a great wheel of cheese and firkins of butter nailed shut too tight for me to open. Barrels of flour and salt are no good to me, but in the back I smell something sweet—something I haven't smelled in so long that I almost can't place it. I tiptoe to the back and pry up the lid.

Apples!

There was an apple tree by the crossroads where Kathleen and I took school in secret. The tree had apples of gold with red speckles, great drooping branches full of fruit. Now Kathleen's a proper scholar and would have walked across an ocean of fire for school. But me? Well, sometimes I'd just go for those golden apples. And I'd bring them home by the armload for Ma and Granny and all my brothers.

I stick my head right into the barrel and breathe in the sweet tang of the fruit. Sometimes when Packy or Christy found work, they brought home flour. Sometimes John did the lord's milking and churning and got a portion of butter for pay. Then we'd have bread and apples for dinner instead of potatoes. Didn't I feel like a king on those days? If Da had still been with us, I wouldn't have had a sorrow in the world.

I reach in and draw out an apple. My hand shakes and my mouth waters as I tuck it away in my coat pocket. I should go. I should creep away, back to Granny. I've got what she needs, but I haven't had an apple in a year. It's been nothing but ship's rations and workhouse gruel and whatever we could beg on the road. The barrel calls to me again. My apple is red and wrinkled. I should put it back, but I tell myself I'll just smell it.

The trouble with hunger is that when there isn't any food at all, you can tell yourself you don't need any and half-believe it. But as soon as the smallest morsel goes in your mouth, hunger wakes up in you like a wild creature. I sink my teeth into the apple and feel the burst of tart sweetness like a bolt of lightning that dazzles your eye and leaves you blind.

I bite and chew and gasp, licking the streams of juice that run down my chin. The honey goodness of it fills me up. Without thinking I start doing the shuffle-hops of the light jig, just for the joy of having food in my mouth.

"Aye, who's there?" comes a gruff voice from the passage.

I freeze, apple juice running down my chin.

"Show yourself."

A sailor brings the lantern to the door of the brig. He's broad-shouldered and black as a bottle of ink. He rattles the chain. I silently slide to the floor. There is a long pause. My heartbeat can be heard from one end of the ship to the other, I'm sure of it. The man gives the nearest barrels a shake.

"Rats scatter when I shake the barrels."

A key snicks into the lock and the chain clanks free.

"There's an easy way to do this and a hard way." He pulls back the hammer of a pistol until it clicks.

My mind snaps back to Packy and the bloody back wall of the police station. The English caught him stealing food, they say. They never proved it in a court. Never had to. Not to shoot an Irishman.

Would this sailor shoot a boy? He doesn't look English but he sounds like them. I raise my hands above my head, above the barrels, and slowly, slowly, I stand up.

"Ahh, for pity's sake!" The sailor lowers his pistol. "Look at the state of you. You're barely thicker than a stalk of wheat. Did you stowaway?"

I shake my head vigorously. My heart runs like a rabbit. He could shoot me right here and they'd never know what became of me.

"I'm only ranked to mete out discipline to rats. The captain will see you for this."

The ship's contract has a litany of flogging offenses. Stealing food tops the list. The sailor takes hold of the scruff of my jacket and steers me before him. Every step of the way I remember my Packy—shot for stealing food. My Da—sent clear to Australia for stealing food. Ma, Christy, and John, all gone and me the last man to carry on the name. I'm going to die on the wide ocean where they won't even set a gravestone over my body—all for the taste of an apple.

The captain's cabin is a lord's estate all packed into one room—candlesticks and shining pewter on the table, maps and pens and inks on the desk. Books in the cabinets and food. Food on the table, a mountain of it between the captain and the quartermaster. The sailor stands in the door.

"Found him in the stores, Captain."

"A thief!" the quartermaster says.

"Who left the stores unlocked?" says the captain.

"Not I," the quartermaster says.

"Chained and locked, sir." The sailor nudges me forward.

"He stole the key then. Shake out his pockets."

I'd been ready to take a flogging if only I could keep Granny's apple. But they'll find it for sure if they search me, and then I'll get a double flogging and Granny'll get nothing.

"I d–don't need a key." Hands clenched, I make a quarter-turn, so the captain can see that I'm thin enough to slip through the bars.

"Christ Almighty! How can I be expected to keep these dregs of humanity alive when they're starving before they set foot on the ship?"

"It's a flogging offense, captain. Won't be a crumb left for us if we let them have their way with the stores." The quartermaster glares at the sailor, who's still got me by the collar.

The sailor opens the top of my coat and shirt and pulls it down to my elbows. He turns my back to the captain for the beating.

A year ago, when the police dragged my Packy away, he shouted to me and Christy and John, "Don't ever bow down to them! No matter what they do to you!"

I grit my teeth and stand straight and tall, like I'm getting ready to dance—my brothers shoulder to shoulder with me on the crossroads. A step down the line, each one of us, and then the shuffle-hop-bangs all in time together. Whatever happened, dancing with my brothers beside me made it bearable. I know what's coming. I've seen it before. I won't bow down to it.

The captain's chair scrapes backward. Heavy footfalls cross the room. I stomp my foot for courage. I bang down again on the heel to keep from crying and follow it with a beat from the toe. Again. Heel and toe. And again. Heel and toe, heel-and-toe, heelandtoe, like the roll of the drum that calls soldiers to battle. Faster. Louder. Heelandtoeheelandtoeheelandtoe.

The flogging doesn't come.

"What's that?" The sailor points to the red speckles on my heaving ribs. "Is it the pox?" He edges away.

"Scurvy." The captain puts a hand on my shoulder and presses down to stop me dancing. "When did the hunger come on you?"

My breath comes in gasps. "Last summer."

"The boy will die if we flog him."

Slowly I turn around, arms still pinned to my sides by my shirt.

"We can't just let him go," the quartermaster insists. "There'll be trouble."

"True enough." The captain gives me a hard look. "What will we do with you, little thief?"

It's not my fault I'm hungry. Not my fault the lord threw us off our land. Not my fault my ma and brothers are dead. I don't want to go to America. I want my own cottage and my own farm and my family round about me.

"We'll run out of food if we let them steal and don't make them pay," the quartermaster says.

"We won't," the captain says, sadly. "That cough you hear from the hold night and day—it's typhus."

A shiver of dread passes straight through me. Bad enough are the English you can see. Typhus is every bit as brutal, but you can't see it coming. The captain goes on in a weary tone.

"We'll lose twenty of them by the end of the week. Maybe forty. So no, Quartermaster, running out is not my chief concern." He turns to me. "But we can't let it be known you stole food either."

He grabs my shirt collar and pulls it back up to my shoulders.

"You and your family will spend the rest of the voyage on deck," he says. "Away from gossip and plotting below and away from the temptation to steal again."

I nod slowly, thinking about how cold the wind blows on the North Atlantic and all the rain.

***

Kathleen comes staggering out of the hold, Granny slung over her shoulder like a parcel, bundle in one hand, case in the other. She'd rather make me watch her struggle than take help from my hand when she's angry.

"What have you done to us, you dirty caffler?" she says, spitting venom.

I take the case and the bundle to spite her and lead her toward the water barrels.

"'*This berth is forfeit,*' the man says to me. Forfeit! After we paid so dear for the passage." She cuffs me upside the head. "Was it not bad enough for Granny before? Do you have to make her sleep on the deck like a chicken in a coop? Are we to be nothing but livestock now? I will crack your head open and scramble your brains."

She goes on in this vein for the whole long walk from the galley door. Near the bow there's space between two water barrels and the side of the ship. She slides Granny from her shoulders, cradles her in her arms for a moment, and then props her up between the barrels. She flutters about Granny like a moth who can't stop circling the candle.

"Go! Find us a blanket or I'll box your ears so hard, you'll not hear a church bell for a month. Do you hear me, little man?"

The black sailor is waiting at the door of the hold, and he's still got that pistol in his hand.

"You'll not set foot below."

In truth, I'm not sorry. It's a relief to be out. The blankets were lively with bugs. I half-expected my covers to crawl away from me in the middle of the night.

I turn up my collar, but my coat and all its patches are no match for the March wind that comes singing out of the north with sleet in its teeth.

"Your captain didn't want me to die of a flogging," I say. "He won't want me to die of the cold either."

I follow him to the sail locker where he fishes out a few tattered specimens for my use.

Back at the water barrels Kathleen and Granny are thick as thieves, wrapped in the one shawl together and talking treason by the look of it.

"Never let them see it." Granny pats the bundle resting in her lap, "or it's hanged you'll be."

"But how did it save us?" Kathleen says. "I don't know how to—"

"Didn't we always have rent when it was asked for? Didn't we get tickets to America when we had nowhere else to go?"

"I still don't understand."

Behind a barrel is as good a listening post as any.

"Always remember who ye are," Granny says. "Descended of the great bards of old. Honored by princes near and far they were. Sought out for music and for counsel. Keepers of history. Writers of songs." Granny leans even closer to Kathleen. "Richer than kings they were, for they made a king's feast merry and bound up his sorrows with sweet music."

"That was hundreds of years ago. What difference could it make now?"

"What difference?" Granny gives Kathleen a pinch. I love that! "What difference? They endured! They swore to remember. Spent their own blood to keep it safe. Whatever happens to you, don't you ever hang your head, no matter how they try to shame you. Don't let them who have sacrificed to keep this treasure for you die in vain."

Kathleen weeps a little but Granny keeps at her, making her place her hand on the little bundle and swear on the names of Jesus and Mary that she'll defend it. I come out of hiding when she's done.

Granny looks up at me with a smile to warm an icicle on Saint Stephen's Day. "Here's himself," she says. "What have you brought me?"

I tuck the torn sails around the two of them. When they are good and settled and the moon is rising and the crew is busy elsewhere, I take the apple out of my pocket and put it in Granny's hand.

"An apple at the end of winter," she says, amazed. "Did the fairies give it to you?"

Kathleen gives me a look to peel paint off a wall. She's figured out how we come by our present luxury accommodations. The minute Granny's not looking, I'll be paying for it in bruises.

"The fairies, of course!" I say, only to peeve her. She hates when Granny goes on about all the things the hedge master called coarse and pagan.

"You can hear them," Granny says. "In the riggings." She nods toward the tall masts and sails and ropes. "It's the fairy wind. They've come for me at last."

"Eat it," I say. "You'll get better. All you need is good food and clean air."

She takes the apple in her weather-spotted hands and breathes in the smell of it. But then she hands it back.

"I remember the taste of apples," her voice gets dreamier by the moment. "I'm past all that now. You mustn't cling to me."

I do cling to her. Tight as I can, me on one side and Kathleen on the other. I sing to keep them away—every hymn I know. Sing because I can. Because it's all I have to give. We sing together straight through the night until the coldest, darkest part right before the sun swims up out of the sea.

The fairies get her anyway. Between one breath and the next, she's gone.

That morning, seven bodies are brought up from the hold. Prayers and wailing come from the open door. Kathleen and I have said the prayers for the dead so many times, we don't need a priest. We wrap her body in a bit of sailcloth.

"Eternal rest grant unto her, O Lord," Kathleen whispers.

"And may perpetual light shine upon her," I answer.

There's no holy water to hand, so we mark her brow with the morning's dew. She weighs no more than a swan. We stand at the rail and give her body to the sea. Nothing marks her grave but water and sky. We stand side by side at the rail and watch that nothing long after we have sailed away from it.

Kathleen is too proud to cry and I am too weary. She goes back to the barrels and gathers Granny's bundle to her heart and rocks it like a child. I build us a tent of torn sails. We don't speak. Later, under cover of darkness, I take out the stolen apple. Kathleen cuts it in two and gives me the larger half. I eat it—slowly this time—and all the sweetness is lost to me.

* * *

Every morning for a week, more bodies are brought out of the hold and buried at sea. For a week, Kathleen and I huddle underneath the torn sails, between the barrels, between Ireland and America, under the weight of all we have lost. We hardly speak. But in line for the daily ration, Kathleen pesters every woman on the ship about her plans. Where will she go? How will she find a job? Some have kin to meet them, or a letter from an employer. Everyone's heard or read about the best place to go.

"Brooklyn—by the Navy yard," says one.

"Manhattan—above Sixtieth Street, where there's land enough to keep a pig and chickens," says another.

We'll land at a place called Castle Garden, they say. The nearest Catholic church is St. Peter, they say.

Every day I stand at the forward-most point of the ship, looking for castles and gardens and St. Peter himself unlocking the doors to America for us. Every day when we get our bread, Kathleen breaks hers in two and hands me half. She watches me eat every crumb of it, and my own portion as well, like a hawk watches chickens. Queen Elizabeth herself was never such a tyrant, and I'm her only colony.

When the first sea birds fly in from the west and circle the masts, a great cheer goes up.

Nobody dies that night.

CHAPTER 2

THURSDAY, MARCH 26, 1863

Landfall comes in the morning. Everyone else crowds the landward rail. Kathleen is a whirlwind at the news. The ruffian has me bent over a cup of cold water, and since there's no soap, she scoops a handful of wet sand out of a bucket and scrubs my face and neck and knuckles with it. Christ never washed me of my sins with such vigor. She finishes scrubbing only a moment before my skin gives way to bleeding. She tosses aside her washrag and takes my freezing wet hands in hers.

"We got this one chance, Danny," she says putting aside her usual vinegar for a motherly tone. "It's a fresh start for us. I'll get a job. You'll go to a proper school. An indoor school with a roof and walls."

"Won't they know we're Irish?"

"They'll know at first," she says. "But we'll fool them. We'll learn to talk and dress and work as they do. And then it won't matter that we're Irish." She twines her thick brown hair into a braid and then winds it up in a knot, fixing it tight with the one hairpin Ma left her.

"I want you to look a proper American. Put on your best shirt."

"This is the only shirt I got."

"Jesus, Mary, and Joseph! What have you done to your other shirt?"

"Nothing! I outgrew it."

"Outgrew it?" She flicks me on the ear. "He outgrew it!" she says to the air around her. "The cheek of him!" She grabs hold of my un-flicked ear and pulls me nose to nose with her. "If you grow another inch, I'll hide you. Don't think I won't! Grow, indeed. Stand up, now!"

I stand for inspection like a regimental soldier. She looks me over with a keen eye, muttering the whole time. "Does he imagine I can pick a new shirt for him off a tree? I won't have a tall brother. See if I stand for it."

Just to spite her I say, "I will grow taller. I will. And then I'll stop wearing shirts altogether, just to shame you."

She commences with the folding of the arms and the tapping of the foot that always comes before an outbreak of violence. We opt for a stare-down this time and then a tactical retreat.

"You'll do," she says from her corner. "And me? Is my dress in order? Do I look old enough for a respectable job?"

She gives a slow turn in the same faded skirt and shawl she's worn every day for the last two years. She looks the same to me—as common as any girl of sixteen years.

"You look a proper spinster," I say firmly. "You could be twenty-five. With a cane and a squint I believe you'd pass for thirty!" I fix her with my best grin, the one with dimples.

"You are the devil's own child," she says, laughing at last. "I will murder you in your sleep one day."

I believe her. I have a nightmare where she murders me in cold blood once a week like clockwork.

We join the rest of the passengers at the landward rail as New York City rises up out of the water. There's been talk below about the war between the

North and the South, most of it wild speculation. We half-expect warships and battalions of soldiers in the streets. But if there is an army in the city, it's completely overwhelmed by the traffic of goods and souls everywhere I look. One tower after another, four stories tall, even five, rises up out of the fog. Flocks of boats choke the harbor. Great slow paddle-wheelers carrying a hundred men churn past a skiff carrying two.

"There's Brooklyn!" comes a cry from a shipmate.

"And Governor's Island!" shouts another.

"New York, dead ahead!"

"Will you look at the size of the place?"

"Pray you don't end up down that way," Sour Nan says to Kathleen with a knowing look. "Black-well's Island." Nan has put on airs the whole voyage long, with her vast knowledge of the city, courtesy of a wealthy cousin who sent for her. "There's a poorhouse on Blackwell's Island," she says.

I don't even need to look. Every time I close my eyes the damp walls are all about me, the windows with iron bars, the rats, the sour water, the bread so stale it made your throat bleed to swallow it, and worst of all—night and day—the sound of people crying. Kathleen slides a hand into mine. Ma and

Christy died in the poorhouse, and John died on the road there.

She stands up straight and squares her shoulders to Nan. "Is that so?"

Not a flinch, my Kathleen. Iron-hearted, she is.

"They call it an almshouse in America," Nan says. "But the treatment's the same. It's crammed in there with the penitentiary, the fever hospital, and the lunatic asylum. Oh, and there's a workhouse too," she adds sweetly. "For orphans."

"Well, now," Kathleen says, dripping ice. "If I were a minor child coming to New York with nothing but a letter to connect me to some shirttail relative I'd never met before, I might be concerned. But a spinster schoolteacher of twenty years is perfectly equipped to care for a younger brother."

"You are not a day older than me."

"Shall I quote the quadratic equation or will you be content with a recitation in Latin?" Kathleen lies, cool as you please. If words were knives somebody would be missing a nose and both ears by now.

"I'm sure you'll do fine in New York," Nan says. "They have a great need for teachers among the lower classes." She lifts her nose in the air and moves down the rail from us.

"She's a ray of sunshine," I mutter.

The whole weary walk to the docks in Cove, I only thought to get here. Granny said America was our only hope and I believed her. But everyone aboard has somebody to call on in New York. Someone to give them a foothold. Kathleen and I—we're all that's left. Ma's brother and sisters died in the Great Hunger. Pa's only brother fled Ireland in a ship that never came to port. Lost to the waves, every soul aboard. I wish I was sixteen—twenty, even—big enough to earn a man's wage. I wish we hadn't sold Da's tools. How will I find proper work without them? Da's tools were sound. Any carpenter looking for an apprentice could see their value. Ma held them back to the last. Carried them out on the road with us. It wasn't until John was burning with fever that she took them in trade for medicine, weeping to let go of the plane and the square and the hammer, like she never wept over her wedding band. Without Da's tools I've got no start in life.

"I'll get a job." Kathleen says. She has such a set to her jaw, standing there like a prizefighter on the edge of the ring. The whole burden of it falls on her. And me, too young, too short, too twelve-years-old to help her. If we'd been ashore, she'd sink a foot into the earth from the weight of it all. I take a deep breath and force some cheer I don't feel.

"Course you'll find a job," I say, flashing the dimples at her, since it's all I've got in the way of lifting people up. "By this light, I take you for a woman of forty. If you'd only let me knock out a tooth, you could be fifty."

Once we tie up at Castle Garden, the general chaos of packing up gives way to complete bedlam. There is no castle and not even a hint of a garden at the bottom of the gangplank. The songs all say the streets are paved in gold. Mud and gravel is all I see. Kathleen lifts her chin to the whole of New York and steps ashore. She clamps a hand on my shoulder.

"If you like the current position of the nose on your face, you'll not stir one inch from my side, Daniel O'Carolan," she says to me. The warrior princes of old Ireland did not have such a grip. You could crack crab shells or the skull of a baby in that grip.

We wait in line for the inspector. He's a weary whisker of a fellow who checks us off a long list.

"Occupation?" he wheezes at Kathleen without ever glancing up from the page.

"Schoolteacher," she says, because a wish ain't the same as a lie.

"Age?"

She pauses to take breath. Sin is no small thing in Kathleen's book. "Nineteen," she lies, bold as you please.

"And the boy?" He points with his pen.

"Fifteen." she says, promoting me the same three years. I rise up on my toes.

"Sickly then, is he?"

"I am not!"

"You hain't seen the worst of it, lad. Keep out of the Five Points if you want to live another week. Next!"

We push out into the crowd at dockside, an ocean of people dashing this way and that. Weather-worn Irishmen cart bales of cotton off one ship and carry bolts of cloth onto another. A man with black hair and a dirty apron pushes a cart of milk cans, singing out, *Milsch, latte, bainne.*

A gang of ruffians with clubs are chasing after a black man shouting "Strike-breaker! Git 'im!" Some folk cheer the ruffians on, but the milkman pushes his cart in the way as they come round a corner and the man slips down an alley amid a clatter of milk cans and a whole lot of shouting.

American relations stand to one side of the

ruckus, weeping for joy, and waving handkerchiefs to us coming down the gangway.

"Nan! My own Nan!" a woman shrieks over the din.

Sour Nan clean knocks me down getting to her cousin. You never heard such kissing and carrying on.

"Oh thank heaven!"

"Look at the state of you!"

"You can't imagine the stench. I'll never be clean of it."

"Here, take my shawl. Are they well at home? Are they alive?"

I'm not in favor of hugs or kissing, but if I'm honest, it pinches me to see Nan walk off arm in arm with a protector of her own, and Kathleen and me buffeted on all sides by strangers with nothing but the one case and the bundle to our name.

A woman in a gray bonnet with a Bible under one arm and a basket of bread over the other calls to Kathleen. "Now miss, are you alone in the world?"

Protestants always have all the food and they are very big on sharing it with us unfortunates. Only you have to swear against God and the pope and say their prayers, not your own, before you eat a crumb.

They're also very big on hauling orphans off to the asylums where you never hear of them again.

Kathleen stands between me and the Bible woman.

"Don't be shy," the woman says. "You'll need a friend in New York. I can help you."

She sounds just like the matron of the workhouse where Ma and Christy died. Kathleen takes a step back, looking for an escape route. The workhouse matron liked to help poor unfortunates, too. She was so helpful, she had the biggest pauper's graveyard in seven counties.

"I have people," she says.

The woman looks pointedly at the families from the boat, who have surged toward a crowd of waiting relatives.

"Give that woman no mind," a bearded man in a dusty top hat says, pressing in closer to Kathleen than a man should. She takes a wary step back from him as well. "It's a job you're looking for, is it not?" he says.

"Job or no, it's the help of good Christians you need." Miss Bible Bonnet is giving no quarter, but Top Hat takes up the argument with vigor.

"You there, man of the house!" A fellow out of

Cork hails me. I turn to see a redhead in a blue uniform. He has a table full of goods—a blue wool coat, two shirts, trousers.

"Was there ever a finer boy for the drum corps!" he says. "You'll sign on with the Irish Brigade. Good to be among your own."

"How'd you know I'm Irish? I didn't say nothing!"

"It's those blond curls, lad. Come now." He beckons me closer and runs a hand over the blue coat on his table. "The whole kit comes with you when you sign on." He unfolds it for my inspection. "And here's a penny just for looking." He drops the coin in my palm. I close my fist. Nobody ever gave me something for nothing before.

I lean over the table. There's a blanket and the clothes, plus a cup, plate, and spoon. And socks! I haven't worn socks in more than a year. And I've never had a shirt that my brothers haven't worn first. Not ever.

"They feed you every day in the army and pay comes every month. Better still, there's a bonus for your family when you sign on. Five dollars for a six-month hitch and ten for a year. We'll teach you to march and play the drum. It's a grand adventure."

Wouldn't I love to put five dollars in Kathleen's

hand. She'd live like a queen on that, milk *and* bread, and every day, too.

"The offer won't last forever," the soldier says. "The draft is coming, and then folk will have to serve without a signing bonus at all. A right-thinking man of the house would join up today. All you have to do is sign." He slides a thick sheet of paper toward me. "An X will do if that's all you got."

I pick up the pen and look sidelong at the page. Reading's a crime in Ireland if you're Catholic. I tap my chin with the pen like I'm thinking it over, but I read the page on the sly.

"It's the Irish Brigade, lad. You'll be among your own. You'll come home covered in glory."

Behind me I hear Kathleen saying stiffly, "A kind offer, thank you, but I won't."

She turns, her skirt brushing my legs, and gasps when she sees the contract in my hand. A claw descends upon my head. Takes hold of my hair. In a flash, I'm three inches taller.

"Drop. The. Pen."

Kathleen is far more terrifying when she's quiet than when she's bellowing. She fixes the soldier with a look to melt iron. "He's my brother. You can't have him."

She lets go the hair, clamps a hand around my arm, and sets a quick march away from the dock.

"He said he'd pay me and it comes with clothes, a blanket, and all."

"Sure and it'll only cost you your life." She pushes her way through the crowd toward the street.

"Food every day says the man." I squirm under her grasp but I might as well be in irons.

"Hundreds of miles from me," she says. "Living among strangers." We dodge around a cart full of dung. "Only to die without a scrap of holy ground to bury you in." She shudders head to foot.

I look behind us. There's a forest of ship's masts and smokestacks tied up at the docks, but between all those rolling decks is the water where Granny lies. Unburied. Adrift forever. I heave a long sigh. I could never. Not for whole plates of food. It'd break her.

Miss Bible Bonnet is speaking to a bald man with a high churchman's collar. She points our way.

"Don't look back." Kathleen plasters on a smile, turns, and waves wildly to a group of complete strangers across the street. "Now!"

We plunge into traffic, hopping over puddles and around the backs of rumbling wagons. We gain the far curb without dying. It's a day full of marvels.

We walk straight through the pack of strangers she just waved to. "This way," she says, still calm and cold.

The shadows of buildings fall over us and the foot traffic thins a bit. We look back to see Miss Bible Bonnet crossing the street after us. Kathleen grabs me by the hand.

"Run!"

CHAPTER 3

We run like dogs, one long block and then two. Buildings tower over us and people swarm the streets. A coal wagon rattles past and children even more pale and ragged than me, children with freckles or maybe the pox, scramble for the dropped coal as if it were treasure. A man in hob-nailed boots pushes a cart full of manure. His face and arms are as deep brown and wrinkled as the trunk of a tree.

Women sit at their open windows with piles of mending in their laps. They have every color of skin from pale as milk to dark as midnight. I didn't know there were so many. I've heard of the black sailors on the waterfront in Dublin. I've even heard of the men with long black braids who come from faraway

China, but I've only ever seen folk who were freckled or not. The women chat with each other out their open windows, laughing at someone's expense on one block, shouting some outrage on the next—their English mixed in with all manner of languages. I could stop and gawk at them all day, but Kathleen tugs me along without mercy.

A grandmother with a basket of apples and not enough teeth calls out, "Three for a penny!" We dodge a knife grinder with a long black beard and a black hat. We cross the street when we hear a fist-fight in a pub. A fine carriage, with a coachman at the reins and a pair of gentlemen dandies inside, rolls toward the harbor. A man with a red beard drives a wagon full of dead fish up town. Another with a cap and apron stands over open barrels of pickles, shouting the virtues of his wares in English and three other languages. Down the alley I see shirts hanging limp on wash lines. Two men wearing long, loose shirts bend over washtubs, stirring them with paddles and stoking the fires underneath. If I stopped to look, I would stand for an hour in one spot while the parade of all humanity swirls by.

We keep going and going, dodging carts and people and garbage, burrowing into the city like a pair of rabbits when hawks are in the air.

As we come around a blind corner, I plow into a blue-eyed woman in a gray shawl with a basket over one arm and a babe in the other. Bread and carrots and potatoes go flying. I stammer out an apology, and drop to my knees to help the woman pick up her food.

"Ye rogue! Ye caffler! Look what you've done!" The woman clutches her babe close to her chest and stoops to collect her goods.

A black fellow with a sailor's kit slung over his shoulder springs to the woman's side with tender concern.

Kathleen and I both bend over to pick up her scattered groceries.

"Go on now, you pickpockets!" the sailor says, putting an arm around the woman's shoulder and raising her to her feet.

"I never!" I say. I take the armful of potatoes and carrots I've picked up and dump them in the woman's basket. I take off my cap to show her respect. Kathleen glances up the alley and down. If they call for a policeman we're done for.

"We have to keep going," she says. She drags me away by the collar.

"I'm sorry!" I call over my shoulder.

"Be careful of yourselves, you young ones," the sailor calls after us.

We dodge from one block to the next, always looking to see if the charity woman is following us. I carry the case and Kathleen carries the bundle swung over her shoulder. It thumps with an odd hollow sound, almost like a drum. She has not let me touch the bundle—not even once. I've been imagining dark magic inside it, old magic from before the church. Kathleen has no truck with the stories, but Granny knew them all, from Finn McCool of old to the fairy folk who still keep their ways and their power in their underground halls.

"This way," Kathleen says, gasping now. She pulls me into an alley, leans hard against a wall, and hugs me tight. "They won't have you, Danny. I won't let them take you."

"Who's taking me?" I squirm, but she won't let go. My stomach's roaring for hunger.

"Orphan asylum, workhouse, they'll take you from me if they think I can't take care of you. I need a job. I need one today."

"The army would pay," I say, wiggling out of her grasp. "Five dollars. Think of it! Ten for a whole year."

I don't want to be a soldier, but I'm solidly in favor of eating every day. She thinks I don't know how light her purse is, but I do. She counts the coins sewed into the hem of her skirt every night. We used to have a farm, a cottage, a cow, and chickens. All gone now—burned. Three pennies is all that's left to us in the world.

"Don't you believe them," she says. "The North is losing the war. Everyone says so. Do you think the soldier on the losing side gets paid?"

"He said I'd be covered in glory."

"Did he now? Well, the villain in the top hat said men would pay me a nickel for a song if I came and worked in his dance hall."

"A nickel a song! That's hardly working." I start counting how many songs I know. "I could do that."

"They're not looking for boys at the dance hall."

"But I know how to dance."

Kathleen lets out a snort of a laugh, but it turns to crying just like that, face in her hands and shoulders shaking.

She never cries. Not in front of me. After a bit, I lean in and let her hug me again 'til the tears are spent. She scrubs her nose with a kerchief that hasn't seen soap in a month and then I hold out my penny.

"Buy you an apple? I saw a lady back there. Three for a penny, one for you and one for me and one for someone worse off than us."

Da used to say that. No matter how little we had, he'd always save a pinch of something for a body who had life worse. Big-hearted and thick-headed Ma called it, but everyone loved him, even her.

"Save it." Kathleen says, closing my hand around the coin.

"But I'm hungry now!" I shouldn't be such a baby. But there you have it. A boy gets hungry.

"We'll find a church," Kathleen says firmly. "The priest will know where an honest girl can get a meal."

At the end of the alley there's a sign. Church Street. Like the angels put it there just for us.

"Come on," I say. "How far can it be?"

Turns out, pretty far. The first church we come to is an Anglican affair with a tall square tower like a prison. We give it a wide berth. Three blocks on we come to a corner with five streets going off in different directions. Kathleen looks down one block and then the other. I can't stop looking at the paving stones. Five triangles of pavers point at each other across the gravel streets.

"Look!" I tug at Kathleen's sleeve. "It's the Five Points the man warned us about."

Kathleen rubs her back under the bundle. "Lord, help us," she mutters.

We've made three wrong turns, I've heard six different languages, and I'm yawning and dragging my feet by the time we see the gray columns of St. Peter. The soup kitchen must be nearby. Wouldn't you know, Kathleen insists we go pray first.

I complain bitterly up all eleven steps and Kathleen has me by the ear on the last three. But when we push open the tall door, she lets me go with a gasp. On the outside, the church is nothing but plain gray blocks. Inside, it's a jeweled wonderland—altars and side altars with gleaming white linens and marble. The Blessed Mother stands in her usual spot crowned in gold and your man Joseph holds Jesus on the other side. There are a few penitents kneeling in prayer; one is piously snoring.

The noise of the street falls away as the door swings shut and the sweet smells of candles and incense settle on my weary shoulders. There's no church so fine as this in all of Ireland, except the ones we aren't allowed into.

I haven't had a heart for praying since Granny died, but the tall, tall ceiling and the colored light streaming in through the window make me want to pray. I slide into a pew at the back and take in the brilliance of it all.

"Daniel! Will you look at this," Kathleen whispers.

Two handbills are posted on the back wall.

Domestic Girls Wanted
Only clean and godly girls accepted
Experience and references required
$1 a week plus room and board

"You've found it!" I say. "A dollar a week, and they feed you!"

"I know," Kathleen says sadly. "It would be perfect." I never heard her so downcast. "Here's the trouble."

The second handbill shows a row of the cleanest red-haired boys you'll ever meet and a great gleaming train beside them. Rolling hills surround them with green fields of wheat and barley and apple trees. The Blessed Mother beams down at them from the corner of the page.

A Bountiful Future
Clean and Healthful Farms
Loving Catholic Families
Share your many blessings with farm families in need.

The boys have round cheeks and straight backs; they look happy.

"Don't you see how it is?" Kathleen says, near to crying again.

"I don't."

"It's no use!" she wails.

"It's a job," I say. "Just like you wanted. And a place to live, too. What's the matter with you?"

"For girls, Danny. They won't take a boy into service."

"Well, all right then. It's the train for us and a Bountiful Future on a Clean and Healthful Farm."

"I'm too old for that train. They want little charmers like you who have years and years in them to work the land. They'll take you from me and keep you forever."

My sister is the plague of my life. I can feel the sting of every time she's pinched me and the lash of every harsh word. I'm never good enough, no matter what I do. But in the wide world, she is all I have.

"I swore that I'd keep you safe. Swore an oath to God I'd never leave you." Kathleen says in that no-retreat voice. "I'll stay right here on my knees. I won't budge from this church until God tells me how to keep you."

My heart sinks down into the deepest, emptiest pit of my belly. This could take long past dinner. In all those Bible stories, Jesus prays clean through the night. And what if God doesn't come through? What if, in all the world full of starving people, the troubles of one sister, and her brother who's a slacker when it comes to prayer, don't earn you a hearing with the Almighty? Kathleen is the sort of believer who believes more the less evidence there is. She could be on her knees for days on end. I'm going to die of hunger while she prays to save me from a bountiful future.

"Would it kill you to have faith?" she says, seeing clean through me.

I hop from foot to foot on the fork of that question. Lie and I'm a sinner. Tell the truth and I'm a heathen.

"What about Granny's bundle? She said it has magic powers. She said it will save us."

Kathleen turns to me sharpish and I remember that I wasn't supposed to hear that conversation.

"We'll be doing no such magic tricks. Powers indeed! Ye heretic!"

She glowers at me and goes to her knees, head bowed, shutting me out with her devotion. The bundle she sets on the stone floor beside her. I'm itching to pick the thing up and tear off the cover. What's the point of having a treasure you don't use?

I slide to the far end of the pew and sulk. Maybe if I pray she'll have pity on me and give our treasure a try. I slide onto the kneeler, fold my hands, and put on my most angelic expression. After an eternity I cut a glance at her and she's not even looking at me. What's the use? If only there was a patron saint of those afflicted by tyrannical sisters there'd be hope for me.

Just about the time I've decided I'm the most miserable boy in all of New York, she reaches in her pocket and pulls out bread. "Take it," she says. "If you make a sound or leave crumbs, I will take that candlestick there and clout you over the head with it." She gives a nod to a polished brass affair, tall as me.

I start to break the roll in half but she puts a hand over mine. "I won't," she says. "I can't."

The bread is as big as my hand. I never had so much for only myself.

"Go on," she says softly.

It has two slashes across the top, just like the ones that tumbled out of the basket of the woman with the gray shawl. I gasp.

"You stole this bread!" I whisper. "In broad daylight! And you're giving it away right here in front of the Blessed Mother!"

I love to make her squirm.

"If I can't feed you, they'll take you from me," she says. "And I swore to keep you. There's nothing I won't do to feed you."

She takes her sins seriously, my Kathleen; I should stop tormenting her. I hold out half the bread to her again. She closes her eyes and rubs her temples with a weary sigh.

"Go," she says even more softly. "Eat. Please."

It's the smell of the bread that persuades me to stop torturing her. It's one handful of heaven. I walk in a trance toward the confessional door. Inside there's a board to kneel on, a cross, a screen, and the most beautiful stretch of clean dry floor. Not pitching in the waves. Not crowded with the bodies of strangers. Not crawling with bugs and mice. Empty floor. All for me. I turn back to my sister.

"Thank you," I say, but she's already gone to the

44

Blessed Mother, hands folded, begging like our lives depend on it.

I was going to pray first. I was going to savor every nibble for hours. But when the confessional door swings shut, I fall on the bread like a starving dog. I bite off as much as my mouth can hold. The feeling of it—cheeks bulging out, teeth crunching on the crust, great warm lumps of bread going down my throat. My heart races and I gasp for breath. I lean against the wall and slide down to the floor. I take another bite and another. There is a grace for after meals but I can't remember it. There is no cold draft under the door. No stench of sewage. I pull off my shoes and put my cap over them for a pillow. In less than a minute, I'm asleep in the bliss of a full belly.

I should have kept a closer eye on her. Who would have thought, there in a church, under the eyes of the angels and saints, she was thinking up fresh tortures for me.

THE INVASION OF KENTUCKY
The Rebels Advancing Toward
the Kentucky River
Brisk Skirmishing in Progress
Various Estimates of the Strength of the
Confederate Force

—*New York Times*

CHAPTER 4

FRIDAY, MARCH 27, 1863

When Kathleen raps on the door, I swim up out of dreams glad to leave them behind. Ever since the landlord burned our cottage and threw us out, I've dreamt of food and nothing else. But last night me and my full belly dreamed of home. Everyone was there. Potatoes in the kettle. Ma and Kathleen mending the landlady's linens. Da and us boys singing. Granny telling stories, and my Packy dancing on the hearthstone. Dream of food and you wake up full, even if it's only for a moment. But dream of home—I never woke up so empty.

"Get up," Kathleen says. It's dead quiet in church.

"It's still dark," I say, yawning and stretching like a cat. "Where will we go?"

"Danny," she says softly. "You better sit down."

It's never good news when you have to sit down. But everybody we have is already dead. What could she say that's worse? I settle on one end of the kneeler. Kathleen slides the case and the bundle in and wedges herself onto the other end.

"I found a way to stay together." She fixes her gaze on the luggage but she's looking much farther away than that. "We'll be safe. But you're going have to listen to me, Danny, like you never listened before. You're going to have to do what I say."

I don't like the sound of it. I check her hand and sure enough she's got the thimble, ready to thump me behind the ear if I argue. I edge into the corner where my ears will stand a fighting chance.

"Service is a good life for a girl like me. It's not teaching, but it's a roof over our heads and a clean place to live. I talked it over with Father O'Neil after you fell asleep last night, and he said over at Tammany Hall they can find a good spot for me and my sister. Lady's maid and laundress. Not every Irish girl gets a chance like this, but seeing as I can read and sew and speak proper English and because I promised to go to Mass every Sunday, he wrote me a letter. A letter, Danny! That's like gold when you're looking for a job."

She pauses looking to me for agreement. But I can smell the mouth of a trap. I go back over the plan.

"What sister?"

"You." She doesn't even hedge.

"You're not serious."

"I am."

My heart sinks right down through my stomach and out the hole in my shoe.

"Now, Danny, don't fight me on this. I'm so weary. Sat up all night making over a dress for you."

"A dress?"

"The tan plaid Granny wore."

"You're going to make me wear Granny's dress!?"

"It's your dress now. I turned up the hem and the sleeve. I put pleats in the front so it will fit you around the middle."

"I don't want a dress! We'll never get away with this. Ain't it a crime go around in the wrong clothes? Ain't it a sin to lie? You can't make me do a sin. I won't!"

She flinches. I've got her now; she's always plaguing me with my sins. I pull my cap low over my brow and hug my arms around my shirt.

"Holy St. Joseph right there beside the altar is wearing a dress. Goes down to his feet, pleats and all. St. Peter and St. Paul and all the rest wear just the same. Look for yourself."

My mouth pops open like a hooked fish. I grasp at straws. "Joseph's from the Bible times. That's not fair. It was a thousand years ago."

"Every priest you ever saw in your life wears a cassock that goes clear to the ground and buttons up like a woman's dress."

"A cassock buttons in the front!" I cry out, sensing a path to victory. "A dress buttons in the back. I won't do any shameful wrong-sided buttoning. You can't make me."

Kathleen grabs me by the shirtfront and pulls me nose to nose. "God doesn't care what side you button on! You could be a both-sided buttoner and he wouldn't care!" And then her voice drops to a dangerous low. "You. *Will*. Wear this dress. And say you're my sister. Or I'll never feed you again. Or eat myself neither. Are you so stubborn that you're going to die just so you can wear pants in your own grave?"

She lets go of my shirt and fumes. Then she composes herself. She takes hold of my hand, gently for a change. Puts on that motherly tone she trots out on desperate occasions.

"You're so young you probably don't remember what Da said to you before they took him away."

I was five. I remember. But I try not to, because I hate crying every bit as much as I hate being hungry. But Kathleen doesn't care about me, because she says it right out loud. "'*Live. Live to dance another day, Daniel.*' That's what he said to you."

I turn to the wall and sniff back snot. I won't let her see me cry. She opens the case and takes out Granny's dress.

"It'll be like a game, Danny. You already know how to walk like a girl. Don't think I didn't see you pantomiming Sour Nan to the sailors so they'd laugh."

True as charged.

"In all the old plays, men acted the women's parts, dresses and wigs and painted faces, even. You'll be a grand actor. You know you will."

The sailors loved it when I did Nan, walking up to the cook and batting my eyes for extra bread, and then sitting up and begging for it like a pup, and then wagging my tail when the cook finally threw me a piece. Had them roaring. I love that sound.

"There will be food. And a roof over our heads."

After the landlord threw us out, we slept in ditches and caves and under trees for months. Our neighbors loved us and fed us in secret, but it's against the law to shelter the evicted, even in a barn.

I run my hand over the polished wood panels of the confessional. "A proper room, not a stable?"

"Not a stable."

"They really won't guess I'm a boy?"

"Daniel. When you dance and sing, you and your blond curls, the whole world smiles at you. You know it's true."

After Ma and Christy died in the poorhouse, we ran away with Granny. We walked for weeks to get to Cove. When we passed a pub, I'd go to the bar and ask, could I sing a song for Ireland? And I'd sing one of them tunes the men who fought the wars like. And someone would break out a whistle or a fiddle and I'd dance a step or two on the bar. It was good for a scrap of food from the kitchen and a spot on the floor to sleep, so long as we moved along the next day.

"People see what they want to see," Kathleen says. "Give them an honest day's work and they won't ask questions. They won't want to know the truth."

I reach out and touch Granny's dress. My brothers would laugh at me if they knew, but not Granny.

She was fierce. More than one time in those pubs, she'd seen a man try to grab me in the back room and come after him with a knife. She'd do whatever it took to save me—even this.

"Stand up and let's have a look."

Kathleen holds the dress up to me. "A good length. Do you want to keep your own clothes on underneath?"

"Can I do that?"

"Can you keep a secret?"

I nod. She lifts up her own skirt a bit and sticks out an ankle.

"You stole Christy's pants?"

"Don't tease me, Danny. Please. He's not needing them and I was so cold in the poorhouse. I begged the matron to let me pray for him one last time before they buried him and she said yes and—oh Danny, I'm so tired of being cold and hungry. I'm tired of being tired. We have this one chance."

She holds the dress out to me with a pleading look.

Angels in heaven help me. I put on the dress right there in the confessional.

CHAPTER 5

We set out from St. Peter in a drizzle that has our clothes damp through before we walk a block. At first I feel as if every eye is upon me and my grandmother's dress, but the crowds are even thicker than yesterday. Workmen in boots clomp along the street toward the ships. Two men from China sit with a barrel between them—one speaks while the other writes with a brush and ink. A woman paces back and forth to shush her wailing baby. Nobody looks at me but I can't stop looking at them.

Down one alley there's the sound of a dogfight and a ruffian with a patched eye collecting the bets. Great barrels of stout go rolling down the wagon ramp and into the basement of a pub. A fat sow roots through the carrot tops out back of a grocery store—a whole pig in the middle of town and nobody snatching it up to feed his family. Folk here must eat like lords to let such a feast go by.

Kathleen tugs at my hand to keep me from falling behind. Her tatter of a handkerchief is pressed over her nose for the stench. A boy near my age—but wearing pants, I notice with considerable envy—nudges and bumps his way through the crowd. And then right in front of my eyes, he slips a hand into a lady's bag and comes out with folded money. Straight away I put my hands to my pockets and run into skirt. A skirt with no pockets. No wonder women get stolen from, money flying loose in their handbags and not in pockets like any right-thinking man would do. I pat the skirt front until I can feel the penny underneath in my pants pocket.

Kathleen bats at my hand. "Girls don't scratch their privates!"

More bad news.

I've got a powerful hunger, and I've never had a whole penny of my own to spend how I like. I peek into the grocer's on the corner. I drag my feet going past the pub.

"Keep up!"

Kathleen gives my arm a tug so I wiggle free of her. She's fixed on reading street signs. A woman hanging clothes in the alley is humming the sweetest tune I've heard in ages. It's slow and sad, and without thinking I step into the alley to give it a better listen. On the second time through I hum along. A good song works on me like a magnet to iron. I don't mean to be loud, but the woman looks up from her washing.

"Where's your ma?" she says. "A pretty thing like you. You'll break her heart wandering off."

I look up, down, and sideways before I realize the pretty thing she's talking about is me.

The woman puts a hand to her aching back. "Run home to your people now, you and your angel voice. 'Taint the neighborhood for a little girl to be lost in."

I look over my shoulder in sudden panic. Kathleen was right there a minute ago. Was it a minute? When a song catches me, time vanishes. Oh, if she thinks I've run off she'll pick me up by the heels and swing me like a cat.

I dash down the street looking for her gray dress and dark hair but there's a sea—a very ocean—of dark-haired women in dresses so smudged they're all gray no matter what color they began.

Panic stabs me. I can't lose her.

At the corner there's a grocer, and I spy an empty crate under a table full of cabbages. I slide it out and climb on top. I stand on my toes peering over heads. Folks swarm in every direction. Even if I could see Kathleen in that crowd, how would I get her to see me? How could I be so foolish to let a song catch me here among all these strangers?

I stomp my foot to keep from crying. The crate has a nice bang to it. I stomp again, my heart racing harder. I don't know how to make her see me, just me, among all these millions, but I know how to get people to look.

I put a reel tune in my head and count out a measure. I start with simple shuffles and bangs but the skirt throws me off. I hitch it up and try again. The crate wobbles if I get close to the edges, so I do the whole step in one spot like Packy taught me. He used to collect bets for dancing on a barrelhead at the pub on a Saturday night.

Soon enough a boy walking by stops to watch, and then a fishmonger leans against his shop door, wiping his silver-smudged hands across a leather apron. A few more stop and the clapping begins. That's what I'm counting on, the clapping in time. It works like a charm.

"Margaret O'Carolan!" Kathleen shouts to me, using our mother's name. She shoulders her way through the crowd with the vigor of a prizefighter. "Come with me at once!"

I flinch, knowing the hiding I've got coming, but she simply holds out her hand to me, calm as can be, while I hop down from the crate.

"I'm sorry," she says to the grocer. "Won't happen again."

"Well now, I don't hold with street jugglers, but this little feather of a girl's not going to harm my boxes, are you?"

"No sir," I say with a bow. And then, remembering the skirt, I dash off my best shot at a curtsey. Kathleen schooled me in the dark art of them before we left the church. It's more complicated than you'd guess: skirts twitched out to the side but not too much, one foot forward, and the bend of the knee just so.

Kathleen takes me by the hand and we walk off together arm in arm like Ma and Granny after church. She doesn't thump me on the head or drag me by the ear. There are hidden advantages to being a girl.

A block farther on and Kathleen says, "Well, here it is."

A gray skeleton of a vast building stands before us. Workers dash every which way with boards and buckets of nails. Men with hods full of bricks up on their shoulders scale ladders taller than a tree. At one end of the skeleton stands a half-finished room. A line of folks winds out the door.

Across the way is a pack of fishermen—anyone could see they're Galway men by the knit of their jumpers. Sturdy fellows and angry. They've got loops of thick rope 'round their shoulders and one is holding a longshoreman's boathook. Shouting and waving clubs they are.

"A dollar ten for a day's labor," one shouts.

"'Tis a disgrace!" cries another. "We're barely living on a dollar fifty."

"And me caring for my brother's wife and kids while he's with the army. It's not to be borne."

"Don't forget the price of goods," shrieks a woman in a shawl from the sidelines. "Rising every day with the war on."

"We won't have it!"

"If we stand firm every man of us, they'll have to give in," shouts the tallest of the men.

"Call your mates. We'll swing together and the hammer will fall hard!"

The men march toward the docks shoulder to shoulder, the sound of their hobnailed boots echoing down the street. A shiver rises. I don't want to be on the wrong side of whatever trouble they're after. Da had many a story about the folk who went out in the dark of night to set right what had been done wrong to working farmers. I'd listen to him with a shiver of fear and pride for what men will do when they've nothing left to lose.

Remembering my Da makes me think of music and the way he'd take that tune I heard this morning and play it for himself. I hum it through once and then again, thinking about where Da would put a trill or little run on his whistle to give the tune some lift. A man farther up in the line with a crutch and an army coat hums along for a few bars and then he sings.

> *Let us pause in life's pleasures and count its*
> *   many tears,*
> *While we all sup sorrow with the poor;*
> *There's a song that will linger forever in our ears;*
> *Oh hard times, come again no more.*

He has a low gravelly voice but it suits the tune, which keeps circling back to the line about hard times. Plain to see everybody here's had their share. Soon the woman behind us is swaying with a baby in her arms and singing along.

> *While we seek mirth and beauty and music light*
>> *and gay,*
> *There are frail forms fainting at the door;*
> *Though their voices are silent, their pleading looks*
>> *will say*
> *Oh hard times, come again no more.*

The man with the crutch gets called into the room. The baby starts fussing, so I pick up the tune, singing it a step up higher than the man. You'd think it would make people sad what with the drooping maidens and lowly graves, but people smile and sway along. Since everyone is in such good spirits I sing a lament or two after and hardly notice when Kathleen takes her turn talking to the big man in the half-built room.

She comes out beaming and hustles me off before I finish the sad ballad of Owen Roe. I'm a little put out; it's a good song. Kathleen waves the little ticket the Tammany man gave her by way of a reference under my nose.

"It's a grand house, the man said." She practically skips for joy. "Three floors of extravagant living and a snug quarter above that for you and me."

I trot to keep up, the skirts making an awful racket around my knees.

"Best of all, I asked for a place as far from the Five Points as we could get and the man was happy to oblige."

We turn left up Bowery Street and keep going. We pass a fire station with a bell up top, its doors wide open, and a gleaming fire engine inside. One fellow in a red shirt and black braces is polishing the brass lanterns on the front and another fellow is painting a snarling tiger on the side. Both of them have blond hair and blue eyes like me. I slow down a bit and I can hear the one fireman speaking to the other in a Dublin accent. I stop in my tracks, astonished. I was sure the fire brigade wouldn't be for the likes of us.

"Girls don't like fire engines," Kathleen hisses in my ear. She tugs at my elbow but the firemen have spotted us now and we freeze in terror. The Cork fire brigade only served the rich swells who paid the subscription every month.

"Good morning to you, miss," the fireman says. He snatches his cap off and ducks his head in

Kathleen's direction. A sudden sunburn flares across his face. Kathleen stares at him like a scared rabbit, the same sunburn a-creeping up her cheeks. I look from one to the other. This is not going to end well.

The older fireman takes in the pair of them and laughs. "Have you moved to the Bowery, little miss?" he says to me.

I nod and Kathleen shakes her head.

The older fireman laughs again. "Whichever it is. Have your father come by the station and we'll line him up with his civic duty—the Fighting Tigers—that's the brigade for a proper Irishman."

"Thank you," I say. "We'll tell him straightaway." I take my arm through Kathleen's to start walking her away. We didn't plan out what to say about our parents. Didn't plan any of this. Kathleen is still flustered and I have to tug at her to get her moving.

"There's a chowder supper," the younger fireman blurts out. "On Friday nights, with dancing and all."

"Good day to you," Kathleen says, remembering her manners at last. She turns and we walk away double-time. When we're halfway up the block I look over my shoulder; the older fireman snaps the younger across the cheek with a polishing cloth.

"Eyes to the work," he growls.

We keep walking. I get hungrier and hungrier as we go and pretty soon I'm eyeing ash heaps for a stray apple core.

"Are we almost there?"

Kathleen peers at the ticket again. "It's right by the new city park," she says. "On Fifth Avenue and Sixtieth Street."

I catch a street sign as we charge past—Bowery and Canal Street. There's a theater wrapped around with scaffolding. A fellow on a ladder out front paints an elaborate gold border around the sign that says Big Al's Variety Show. A man with a gray beard, spectacles, and black hat shows an armful of velvets in jewel colors to a man in a fine coat and fancy silk tie. I turn and stare, imagining what wonders lie inside a theater.

"Pay no mind to it," Kathleen commands, marching me onward. "If it's music you're after, we'll go to church."

There are fewer tenement houses and more workshops and factories as we go north. Machines hum. Great wagons with draft horses pull all manner of goods in and out.

We spy a policeman in the block ahead and hide

in the alley until he passes. Every pub with a pot of soup that we walk past is pure torture. By the time we hit Madison Square and turn onto Fifth Avenue, I could commit murder for a crust of bread.

At last, Kathleen has mercy on me and we part with a coin for a bowl of soup and a slice of bread to share.

"Sit up straight," Kathleen says. "Knees together. Don't slurp. Close your mouth when you chew."

There's no end to the rules when you are eating like a girl. She hurries me through and we hit the street again.

She goes on about the family, Elbridge and Zola Treadwell. He's a war profiteer, the Tammany man said. Something about selling repeating firearms. Frightfully rich. Mustn't cross them ever. The wife knows every household in town.

"Are you sure this house isn't in Canada?"

"There, now," Kathleen says, stopping for breath "We're on Fourty-Third. We're practically there." I glance across the street. There are two buildings with a courtyard in the middle. Clusters of black children in tidy smocks are playing with hoops and sticks, boys on one side of the yard and girls on the other.

"Is this a school?" I say in wonderment. There are a hundred or more children.

"It is no such thing," says a woman in a grand coat with a fur collar. "It's the Colored Orphan Asylum, for those folk too lazy to raise their own children." She lifts her chin in the air. "Some wild Quaker scheme, to lift up those who can't be helped." The woman takes her own child by the hand and walks away without a backward glance.

I can't stop staring into the asylum yard. The orphans aren't pushing a capstan in circles or breaking rocks. There isn't a rat in sight. Nobody's getting punched in the corners of the yard. Real glass windows! No graveyard!

I thought American asylums were going to be every bit as bad as the Irish ones. These kids look fine. Happy even. Nobody's got the pox. Nobody's hunched over and coughing. For sure they look like they get more than half a bowl of soup a day.

"Doesn't look so bad."

"You have to be black to get in there," Kathleen says. "Those Protestants, they make a special case for black folk on account of slavery. All manner of provisions for their improvement, so long as they worship like they're told."

She takes in the view of the children, so much better fed and clothed than us, and sighs. "Well, your man Daniel O'Connell said that a slave is equal in his humanity—equal to us all. There's none better than the great emancipator himself." She sighs again.

I give the orphans and their fine clothes and full bellies a longing look. Maybe it would be worth giving up my immortal soul to live there. Maybe your eternal salvation is not so much to trade for food to eat and medicine when you're sick. Maybe I wouldn't miss my faith if we only had a roof against the rain.

"Besides, you're not an orphan." Kathleen takes hold of my hand and pulls me along the street. "Not while I have breath in my body. Come on. We mustn't keep the Treadwells waiting."

COLORED SURGEONS

The Secretary of War has ordered that Dr. Auguste (the colored man who presented himself a few days ago for examination before the Medical Examining Board) shall be examined by the board preparatory to being assigned to duty as Surgeon in one of the negro regiments.

—*New York Times*

CHAPTER 6

I count streets. "Fifty-eight . . . fifty-nine . . . Is this it?"

We stand on the sidewalk and look up and up and up. Probably Queen Victoria does not live in a house so fancy.

Kathleen mutters a prayer under her breath. She smooths her hair and then fusses with mine. She makes me turn in a circle while she beats every bit of dust out of the dress, muttering all the while about my demented attraction to dirt. It's not my fault. It's the dress that brushes up against things it has no business mingling with. If I were in a proper narrow set of pants, I'd be the cleanest boy you've ever set eyes on. We march up the front step and bang the lion-head knocker. It echoes like a tomb.

"Be good, Danny," Kathleen whispers through her teeth. "For the love of God, be good."

I stand up straight and put on the good smile. A dandy in a coat and tie opens the door. Warm air and the smell of soap and loads of money wafts out.

"Good day to you, Mr. Treadwell," Kathleen says, dropping a neat curtsey. "We are here to inquire about the maid and laundress positions."

The man looks down his long narrow nose at us. He steeples his long narrow fingers directly beneath a lipless frown. "I am Reeve," he says, as if proclaiming scripture from the pulpit. "Servants enter at the rear."

The door swings shut with a click that feels like a slap. I don't know what to say. I was good. In those three seconds, I didn't do a single bad thing.

We go to the corner and turn down the alley. The gravel street gives way to rutted mud. I unlatch the back gate. Tidy rows of vegetable starts line one side of the walk, and a tub full of soaking laundry and empty clotheslines stand on the other.

At the back door Kathleen whispers, "Lord, have mercy on us," and knocks.

The woman answering is barely taller than me with a round face and a round white collar and cap.

"Are you come for the maid and laundry job? At

last! A body can only do so much. Worn to a tatter," she says before we've gotten off a curtsey or an introduction.

"Good grief!" she goes on, hands on hips and glaring at us. "The stench of you! Have you come straight from the boat? You have. With the luggage. Disgraceful. What are you thinking? This is no way to present yourselves. The tattered clothes. You'll never be accepted in this state! Can you speak, child? Do you have a word of English between the two of you?"

"English is all the language I have," I say resolutely.

Granny spoke Irish when she was a child and they beat her for it. She saw to it none of us knew the shame of speaking the wrong language.

I look over the cook's shoulder into an absolute wreck of a kitchen, dirty pots stacked in the sink, vegetable scrapings in a heap, coal bin nearly empty.

"Is all that laundry outside your work?"

"No!"

The woman has a hefty rolling pin in one hand, and I am seized with the desire to stand well back from her in case she takes a swing with it.

"It is *not* my laundry. I am strictly a cook, a better one than the lady of the house deserves. I've cooked for a countess in Aschaffenburg. In a proper palace, if you'd like to know. What is this household coming to? And the grand soirée she goes on about. Who's going to do all the work?"

"We are," Kathleen says. "We've come for the hiring."

"Not looking like that you haven't! It's all appearances with the lady of the house. Why can't those damn fools down at Tammany Hall send us better than the scrapings of the pot?"

"We've come a long way," Kathleen says, fighting to keep the sound of desperation out of her voice.

I can't take my eyes off a loaf of bread and a round of cheese on the table. There's a bin of potatoes and onions underneath and slabs of beef on the chopping block. There's even a pot of tea on the stove. A dribble collects at the corner of my mouth.

"As long as we're here we might as well help you," I say. "Kathleen can scrub a pot like a house on fire. You'll want those clothes on the line before the sun goes down. Am I right?"

"It's for the lady of the house to say are you hired or no."

The cook surveys the washing in the yard with a heavy sigh.

"Let's show her what we are worth, then," Kathleen says. She takes a step toward the sink.

The cook claps her rolling pin into her hand with a firm and menacing smack. "You'll not set foot in this house in those vermin-infested clothes. Out to the laundry with you both. Quick march. Get that wash scrubbed, and whatever you do, show some decorum with the lady's underpinnings."

"Yes, ma'am," we both say.

We pivot on the porch and head for the wash-tubs, me wondering what on earth an underpinning might be and how you figure the right decorum for a stack of laundry. You wouldn't think clothing gets up to much scandal. There's no end to the female mysteries.

Kathleen and Ma used to take in the landlord's washing and mending. I pump a bucket of rinse water, and she commences with the scrubbing. I slosh the soapy clothes in the rinse bucket, run them through the wringer, and pin them up on the line. Kathleen gives me the full bible of rules about washing clothes: which ones are delicate and not to be scrubbed and which ones can be pounded with a rock to get them clean. It's all news to me. Apparently underpinnings are a lady's drawers and the bit that goes over her diddies. They get hung up underneath a sheet or a pillowcase so as to not shock the neighbors.

My arms are aching by the time the washtubs are empty. The cook marches out, still vexed with us.

"I found these in the rag bin," she says. She holds out plain black dresses, well-worn but clean. "They'll do for now. Go change in the washing shed."

Kathleen takes the dresses. She sends me for fresh water while she closes all the shutters in the shed.

"Strip off all your own clothes, even the pants underneath," Kathleen says when I step into the dark of the shed. "Or the smell of them will give you away." She takes a rag from the bin and rubs it on the cake of laundry soap. "Scrub, like your life depends on it."

I won't lie, it feels good to get clean. Even with blinding cold water. Kathleen rolls up my britches and shirt inside Granny's dress and hides them up in the rafters. I pull on the smaller dress. Kathleen turns her back to me as she hustles into hers. She rubs my head dry with a bit of flour sacking and rewinds her hair into a knot.

"May we enter now?" Kathleen calls.

"All right then, Bridget," the cook says.

I look all around for the Bridget she might be talking to.

"Come now, you don't really expect quality folk to remember your outlandish names. Bridget will do. Bridget and Mary."

"But—" She didn't even ask our names.

"You'll get used to it. Folk shouldn't have to remember something foreign."

It's just a name. I shouldn't care. I put my shoulders back and my chin up to show I don't.

The cook walks a full circle around us. Inspects our hands. And then, like a circling hawk, she swoops down on my head and bends me forward to finger through the hair on the back of my head for lice. She makes a satisfied grunt, releases me, and does the same to Kathleen. Next she steers us to the sink. We stand over the washtub and work dishes for ages while Cook tortures us with the smell of roast beef.

"I'll judge the mood of the missus," Cook says at last and heads upstairs with a pot of tea and a plate of biscuits.

We perch on stools in the corner. Only the thought of Cook's rolling pin caving in my skull keeps me from grabbing a potato and stuffing it in my mouth in one go. We hear lively chatter and shoes clicking across the floor above. My stomach makes an un-girlish growl.

"Oh for pity's sake," Kathleen says. She takes the cut-off carrot tops from the scrap pile and gives me one to gnaw. It's only enough to stir up my hunger.

"Up you go," the cook says, three carrot tops later.

We follow her up a stair as dark as a coal mine and steep as a mountain.

"The mister is traveling, which is just as well, but that conniving grasper Mrs. Vanderzanden is lodged in the parlor like a cork in a bottle. Oh, it'll take some greasing to get the woman loose."

I can't guess what we may find at the top of the stairs.

Cook goes on and on. "That Vanderzanden woman thinks she's quality but anyone can see she's on the outs in proper society. Never mind about that. You stand up straight. Answer true. Can you read and write at all?"

"We can," Kathleen says without even hesitating, so maybe it's not against the law to read in America. That's a relief. There's only so many lies a boy can keep up. The dress is already taxing my powers of fiction.

"Is that a fact? Your kind! Who would think it?" Cook rabbits on. " I don't suppose you can sew, given the rags you were wearing."

"I can. Plain work and fancy. Mending and tailoring," Kathleen says with pride. The truth is she hates to sew, but Ma always said a woman with a good needle can make her way in the world.

"Oh indeed. Fine work too. Well, that goes to your favor. I'm worn to a tatter, I say. She has to hire someone. It might as well be you."

We step out into the butler's serving pantry with gleaming china and polished silver and a stack of fine linen napkins. An apple pie rests on the counter. I fix it with the gaze of a courting lover and feel a great pang of jealousy when Cook rushes us into the next room.

CHAPTER 7

The sitting room is a dazzle of gaslights and cush-
ioned chairs and great swoops of velvet curtain.
A portrait of a fair-haired lad in blue uniform hangs
over the fireplace in a gold frame tall as me. A slen-
der woman in a blue dress sits at a tea table with an
older woman in green. The pair of them drip with
lace like a bishop on his throne, and both dresses
are so wide at the bottom you could hide a flock
of sheep underneath, lambs and all. There is a girl
about Kathleen's age with mouse-brown hair sitting
by the window with a book in hand.

"The applicants, ma'am," Cook says to the
woman in blue. "Bridget and Mary," she adds, not
bothering to indicate which is which. "May I present

the lady of the house, Mrs. Elbridge J. Treadwell, and her dear friend Mrs. Charles Vanderzanden. And Miss Temperance Treadwell, at her studies as usual."

We bob our curtseys.

"Fast workers and clean," Cook says. "Checked them for vermin myself. Not a louse on them."

Kathleen winces visibly.

Mrs. Vanderzanden makes a disapproving cluck. "Too young."

"Do you think so?" Mrs. Treadwell looks anxiously from us to her friend. "It's ever so hard to find the right kind of help."

"It will take you an eternity to train them properly."

"Do you have any experience at all?"

Kathleen hesitates, searching for the perfectly correct thing to say.

"I've laundered," I blurt out. "Loads of it!" I ain't lying. Just finished more loads of wash than I've ever done in my life. Mrs. Treadwell perks up a notch so I keep rolling. "I favor the pine-tar soap, ma'am. It is superior in every way for cleaning."

She nods with satisfaction, secure in the knowledge that she's bought the right soap.

"I sew. Plain work and fancy," Kathleen adds. "Mending, darning, and tailoring."

"Oh heavens! They're Irish girls. What a pity. My dear Mrs. Treadwell, trust me. Get a German maid. I've got a German girl. She's a respectable Protestant; never gives me a moment's trouble. You'll have rampant popery if you let these Catholics in. At times like this when our brave boys are tested in the fields of battle, it's vitally important that we have right-thinking and patriotic households."

"Oh dear," Mrs. Treadwell says, looking more anguished by the moment. "The grand soirée is just months away, there's so much to do."

"I'm only thinking of you, my dear. Why, if it weren't for me, you'd be the last woman in the city with black house servants. Can you imagine?"

Temperance looks up from her book with a start. "Mother, you said Martha and Lucy *wanted* to go. Did you dismiss them?"

"Of course they wanted to go. They went to be among their own," Mrs. Vanderzanden says, sly as a cat. "It's so much nicer to be with your own kind. Don't you agree? Your mother only helped them decide to go."

"But I've known them all my life," Temperance says.

"Think how much their own family will have

missed them all this time," Mrs. Vanderzanden says. Butter would not melt in that woman's mouth.

"They don't have any family besides us," Temperance says. Her face goes from sallow to pink. "Martha has been with us forever. And Lucy has been here since Valor was a baby, Mother. How could you let them go?" Temperance gives Mrs. Treadwell a pleading look.

"Temperance, dear, it's time for you to practice your piano."

There is a moment of silence as the three ladies look at each other. I think I can hear one heart break just a little bit.

"Please excuse me, Mother, Mrs. Vanderzanden." Temperance blinks back tears, makes an elegant curtsey, and glides from the room.

"Oh dear," Mrs. Vanderzanden says. "*Spirit.* Such an unfortunate tendency in a young lady. Never you mind, Mrs. Treadwell. You've done the right thing."

"I am so grateful," Mrs. Treadwell says. "You are a true friend."

"Yes, I am." Mrs Vanderzanden leans in and in a stagy whisper says, "And now the distinction of last family with black servants falls upon our dear Mrs. Albers, poor thing."

"I know," Mrs. Treadwell chimes in with glee. "Did you see her at the opera premiere?"

"I did not."

"Was she on the committee for the decoration of the graves of our noble soldiers?"

"Absent."

"The ladies' charitable tea and garden society?"

"Banished."

The pair lean heads together and giggle.

"You shall do so much better than poor Mrs. Albers, my dear. We shall reel in the correct company for your grand soirée and make such an impression."

"Yes." Mrs. Treadwell looks at her friend with all the loyalty of a hungry puppy.

"Between your son's dashing war exploits and your talented daughter on the cusp of entering society . . ."

"She is very talented." Again with the pleading looks.

"Don't you worry. She'll get her proper debut. Golden days are right around the corner."

"I want nothing less than an extravaganza of music and poetry," Mrs. Treadwell says. "I'll be the P.T. Barnum of the arts!"

Her friend releases an airy giggle. "Oh my dear,

80

the things you say! You will be so very much more refined than the colorful Mr. Barnum."

"We'll have a recitation of Mr. Henry Wadsworth Longfellow's lovely rhymes," Mrs. Treadwell says, swelling with pride. "It must be a program to make the society page. All I need to do is find a worthy singer to accompany my Temperance's fine piano. I'll discover a new voice. A golden voice!"

"Excellent notion," Mrs. Vanderzanden beams. "Someone nobody has heard before."

"And then they'll *have* to invite me to join the Opera Guild!"

Kathleen looks from one woman to the other, her hands clasped together to keep them from shaking. "I have a reference from Mr. Tweed himself, ma'am, and a letter of introduction from Father O'Neil of St. Peter."

Mrs. Treadwell looks at Kathleen and then me as if just now noticing that we are still in the room.

"Ah, yes, the maids," she says.

"Whatever happened to your hair, child? It's as short as a boy's."

My heart races.

"We sold it," Kathleen says. "To a wig shop. Blonde fetches more than brown."

"Such a pity when the younger sister is the real beauty in the family," Mrs. Treadwell says.

Kathleen's face starts to pink up. "We need this job, ma'am. You won't find harder workers."

"The Van Pelts next door have an Irish maid. Hardest worker on the block," Mrs. Treadwell says tentatively. "Most of my neighbor's maids are Irish."

"Are you worshipers of the Pope?" Mrs. Vanderzanden cuts in.

"We are Catholic, ma'am," Kathleen says firmly.

"Catholic *and* Irish. It's too great a risk."

There is a snort and a clatter of china from Cook in the butler's pantry.

"Oh dear, that's a shame." Mrs. Treadwell sighs. "Well, off you go then."

Kathleen stops breathing entirely for a moment, but I'm not surprised. The only way to get a decent job in Ireland is to be a Protestant. I guess America's not so different after all. Cook bustles in and shoos us toward the stairs.

"Now, my dear, I must be going." Mrs. Vanderzanden says. "Don't you worry about your soirée. It will be the talk of the town."

The foul creature who ruined our chances gets up and descends the broad front staircase in a swoosh of lizard-green velvet. Cook herds us cruelly past the pie and straight down the narrow stair without even the benefit of a parting sniff.

"That woman," Cook huffs when we've reached the bottom, "is a . . . a viper!"

Kathleen has gone pale. She clutches the edge of the counter. I look at the tower of dishes we've scrubbed for nothing. "She's a whole nest of vipers," I say. "A reptile."

"Not a drop of warm Christian blood in her."

"She might not have blood at all. She could be a clockwork."

Cook claps her hands together in satisfaction. "The clockwork neighbor! So true. And how she winds up the missus. It's a disgrace!"

Kathleen lets out a low moan. "What are we going to do? We have nowhere to go."

"Don't fret, duckling," Cook says. "It's me that's stuck with the work of three women. I'm the one to be pitied. And Reeve too high and mighty to peel a potato or sweep a floor. It's not to be borne. I'll need a drop of something wet to fortify myself. That's just what I'll do. Irish, indeed. She's not so pure."

Cook opens a cupboard, uncorks a jug, and pours out a hearty portion.

Kathleen walks toward the back door in a trance. I grab the slice of bread from the heel of the loaf and smear it thick with butter before anyone says I can't. It's only fair for all that work. I stuff the bread in my mouth and follow her out. Kathleen slumps down on the step, not even crying, just gasping for air and shaking like a fellow who got the bad end of a fist-fight. I gulp down the last bite of bread and lick the crumbs off my hands. Kathleen starts to moan and rock. She draws her arms and legs together in a ball, tears falling.

I stand beside her and pat her head. "*A stór mo chroi,*" I say over and over, whatever that means. Granny used to say it to Ma when she was grieving for Da. It doesn't soothe Kathleen, and I don't remember it ever stopped Ma from crying either. I sing the lullaby Granny used to croon to us. It's a simple thing, the only song I know in Irish. She forbade me on pain of a hiding to ever sing it out of doors, but what could it matter now? We've nothing to lose.

The washerwoman across the fence sets her basket down and stretches her weary shoulders as I sing. The coachman mucking out the stable pauses and leans on his shovel. I lift my voice on the second verse and by the third I'm letting it ring out. A window on the neighbor's house opens and a girl in black with a white apron leans out to listen.

The washerwoman across the fence sways back and forth a-tapping her heart as if cradling some long-gone child.

When my song is done the washerwoman takes a step closer and says very softly, "The woman of the house is watching at the window above. Sing something in English if you've got it. Melt the heart out of her, lad."

The song from the morning has been chirping in my head all day like a little bird. I think of all them folks in line, struggling just like us. I take hold of my sister's hand and sing it out as pure and clear as a hymn in church.

There's a pale drooping maiden who toils her
    life away,
With a worn heart whose better days are o'er:
Though her voice would be merry, 'tis sighing all
    the day,
Oh hard times, come again no more.

Cook opens the kitchen door and stands there with a tall glass of the wet in her hand and a tear in her eye. A bell rings to call her upstairs but she doesn't budge.

> *'Tis a sigh that is wafted across the troubled wave,*
> *'Tis a wail that's heard upon the shore*
> *'Tis a dirge that is murmured around the lowly grave*
> *Oh hard times, come again no more.*

Mrs. Treadwell steps out of the shadows of the kitchen.

"Is it the child singing? The pretty one?"

I take both Kathleen's hands in mine. I look at her with the nearest approximation of sisterly devotion I can muster on the fly.

> *'Tis the song, the sigh of the weary*
> *Hard times, hard times, come again no more.*
> *Many days you have lingered around my cabin door*
> *Oh hard times, come again no more.*

"Oh my stars!" the lady of the house says. "I've found my golden voice."

FROM THE ARMY OF
THE POTOMAC

The Scarcity of Provisions in the
Rebel Army has No Effect on their
Ardor—the Shenandoah
Valley to be Left a Barren Waste

—*New York Daily Tribune*

CHAPTER 8

FRIDAY, APRIL 3, 1863

A week on in the Treadwell house, and I am crawling up to my bed each night, I'm that exhausted. Kathleen is so busy with fitting and tailoring for Miss Temperance that I do most all her sweeping and dusting. And washing the pots for Cook, on top of the piles of laundry. Still, I've got it better than Kathleen. Miss Temperance hates to be fitted and fussed over and her mother delights in nothing more than fussing. It's like standing between artillery pieces in a pitched battle.

To make matters worse, Temperance liked the last maid and won't let Kathleen forget it. All day long it's "Martha did it *this* way. Martha *knew* how to fix my hair. Martha would never choose brown for my complexion." Dresses flung on the floor. Hair ribbons tossed into the fire. I've never seen the like of it.

Mrs. Treadwell's lady's maid, Sophia, watches the whole thing without a word of support or a gesture of fellow feeling. At the hedge school, Kathleen was always the quick one. At catechism on Sunday, she always had the right answer. Here she's wrong at every turn. It takes all her considerable grit not to bust out in a scalding rage.

At least for me, the room is empty when I clean it. Nobody sees me tripping over the hem of my dress. I fell on the stairs twice yesterday and four times the day before that. All her life Kathleen has moaned to me about the sorry lot of women. I'm starting to think there's something to it. Who decided it has to be dresses for girls? And who says they have to come all the way to the ground and drag in the dirt? Pants don't. I've had my fill of scrubbing dusty hems. That's the truth of it.

To be fair, they feed us.

"If I ever catch you licking the bowl like a dog again," Cook said that first morning when she gave me a whole bowl of oatmeal for myself with butter and raisins besides, "I will put a leash around your neck and chain you out of doors. You're a disgrace!"

But she's given me an extra scoop of porridge in the morning ever since. No sugar. She doesn't hold with sugar for the help, but there's always a thick pat of butter and one day, she put on a dash of applesauce. At night there are the glorious leftovers of whatever the ladies of the house are eating—burnt ends of the roast, thinnings of the gravy, heels of the bread, and all manner of boiled vegetables.

I ate myself to a near stupor the first night just in case they decided not to feed me the next day. But they did. I gorged myself again the second night and the third, but after four days I stopped eating long enough to get a good look in the pantry. It has long rows of pork and beans in a can and glittering jars of fruits and pickles and jams. We could withstand a siege of the King's Dragoons for a month in this house.

I know that the fear of hunger will never leave me, not if I live to be fifty. But the roaring agony of hunger has left me in just one week—gone like a summer lightning storm that leaves you drenched and gasping.

Yesterday the lady of the house caught sight of my shoes.

"Are you a field hand?" she fumed at me. "You'll ruin my good floors!" She threw them out on the spot—my own shoes. They were John's before me and Christy's before that. I rescued them in secret and hid them in the shed with my right clothes. Now she has the nerve to scold my bare feet every time she sees them peeking out from my skirt. What did the woman think I had inside my shoes? There's no understanding rich folk.

Kathleen sews long after supper, hunched over her work, thimble in hand, and a candle sputtering on a plate. She makes me sit up with her and take lessons in elocution and grammar. She has me read the thrown-out newspapers aloud. All week the papers have been about the draft. Men twenty to thirty-five, and single men older than that, have to sign up to be in the army, citizens and newcomers like us, too.

She's found a stub of a pencil and uses it to torture me with sums and fractions. I start marking off days to Sunday on the wall, so she won't forget my Sunday rest. A full hour of sitting still at Mass with no one to make you wait on their pleasure—heaven! I never felt a longing for church 'til now.

I keep to myself washing up in the yard. The other washerwomen are full of gossip and I'm in fear of saying something boyish, so I keep my mouth shut in spite of my true nature. Kathleen's the shy one, but she's made a friend in the Bridget who cooks across the alley from us. Her right name is Jane. She speaks like a Corker and is the one age with our ma, so they took to each other straight away. She told Kathleen that St. Francis Xavier is the place for us. Run by the Irish Jesuits, she said. So we won't find a lick of scorn if we show up in our own homespun woolens. Better yet, it's above Fifteenth Street. There's not a lady in any of the grand houses who would let her maid stray below Fifteenth Street for fear of contamination with the blue death or worse.

By suppertime Friday Kathleen is positively humming for joy in anticipation of church. We eat, as always, down in the kitchen at the wooden baking table with its knife scars and dusting of flour.

Cook plunks down bowls in front of me and Kathleen at one end of the table and Sophia at the far end. Kathleen and I cross ourselves.

"Bless us O Lord and these thy gifts which we are—"

"Don't let me hear you pray that popish nonsense,"

Cook snorts. She dishes up a plate for Reeve, who eats in the butler's pantry while the ladies of the house take their after-dinner aperitifs.

I shut right up but Kathleen goes on boldly, but a little more quietly than before. "—about to receive, from thy bounty, through Christ our Lord. Amen."

"It's the lady of the house's bounty that feeds you," Cook grumbles. She motions for me to come carry Reeve's plate upstairs. "It's to her you should be grateful. God has no truck with your kind."

I want no part of that talk. I take the plate and double-time it up the steps. When I come back down they're still at it.

"Why do you suppose the Irish suffer such humiliations? God is punishing you for idolatry," Cook says.

"All have sinned and fallen short of the glory of God," Kathleen quotes firmly, not looking up from her bowl.

Cook doesn't have a ready quote to come back with, so she dishes her own dinner and takes it at the sideboard by the window. I tuck in, giving my full attention to the turnips and peas. Sophia eats slowly, knife-and-forking it the whole time. She's a lady's maid, not a housemaid, which puts her a cut above Kathleen and me. She has a fashion page from the newspaper beside her and she's eyeing the spring bonnets like they are slices of pie.

"Reeve will be down for wages," Cook says sternly to Kathleen. "You'll make your proper curtsey and give him no trouble."

"Be grateful they hired you at all," Sophia says. "Unfit as you are."

Suddenly the gravy doesn't go down so smooth. I lick the spoon anyway, but the dread of not knowing what Sophia is smirking about spoils the savor of it. At last Reeve comes. Sophia and Cook line up so we slide in behind them.

There is none of the cheer I remember from when men back home got paid. They'd jostle around the paymaster of the roads for their due. "Health to the master!" they'd call out when the pay was just. And more often "Mercy upon his soul!" when it was not. And then off they'd go arm in arm singing to the grocer or the doctor or whoever else they owed. I remember the first time Packy put a coin in Da's hand from working the roads. He was ten feet tall that day. If I knew where Da lives in Australia, if he lives at all, I'd send him the full wage straight away just to feel that tall.

Reeve puts a paper note in Sophia's hand. "You're dismissed from church because Mrs. Treadwell will need you to dress her for the opera later. Don't leave the house."

"Thank you, Reeve." She bobs a curtsey and leaves.

Cook's hand is out next.

"Mrs. Treadwell approves of the fish from yesterday and requires more of the spring greens than you showed this week."

"More of the spring greens? More of the spring greens! Does the woman think I command the sun to shine? It's been a cold spring. She can see for herself how the yard garden grows. It goes the same in every yard in all of New York State. Honestly, Reeve. Where does the woman think greens come from?"

Reeve's normally lipless visage puckers into vertical lines. "She thinks greens come from the kitchen. Make it so."

Cook snorts at him like a wayward draft horse.

"Bridget," Reeve says. He drops a single coin in Kathleen's hand. "Mrs. Treadwell is completely worn out with giving you directions. You will learn more quickly if you value your position."

Kathleen makes her curtsey, eyes fixed on the coin in her palm.

"Mary," he says next.

Even after a week I'm not used to answering to that name. He turns to me and I look up. I did not think it was possible for Reeve to look more unhappy than he routinely does.

"I am required to report Mrs. Treadwell's delight with your singing. You will report to the music room for lessons with the maestro starting Saturday afternoon."

"Music lessons?" Kathleen says warily. "For my sister?"

Who has ever heard of a washerwoman taking music lessons alongside the daughter of the house? They don't even let me sit on the chairs. The music room is the fanciest one—"the salon," the lady of the house calls it, in a voice so French-sounding anyone would think she's Napoleon. I try to imagine what a lesson will be like. I've only ever listened until I knew the song by heart. Maybe I'll be put to shame by the music master, but even so, I'm longing to try.

"No good'll come of it," Cook mutters under her breath.

She could be right. My disguise holds mostly because I'm out of sight—washing up in the yard, cleaning empty rooms, scrubbing pots in the kitchen. A music lesson will put me right under their noses.

I should be afraid. Maybe I will be. But I like the sound of the piano when Miss Temperance practices, and I won't lie, I love the notion of an hour in the day when I'm not scrubbing and polishing. It's just singing; what could go wrong?

Reeve puts the smallest coin in all of Christendom in my hand.

"I hear that you eat volumes of food that would choke a horse at an unladylike speed and that you skip about like a goat in a barnyard. We are running a dignified household. You will conform yourself to it."

I know this is the spot where I should to be grateful, but I can't stop staring at the coin in my hand. It's barely a fish scale and thin as paper with no Lady Liberty taking her ease on it like all the other coins. A shield over a star. I flip it over and it's got three bars on it. Three! I look over at Kathleen's.

"Reeve," I say, stepping forward, hand in a fist. "My sister's wage is a seventy-five cents a week. We agreed on it with the lady of the house herself. That's only a quarter."

Reeve's face goes a worrying shade of mulberry and Kathleen puts a warning hand on my arm.

"I worked hard all week. Did all that was asked. We agreed on fifty cents and this is only a trime."

"You ungrateful wretch. A dollar has been taken from your wage for the clothes you are wearing. You will report to the service door of Smith's Dry Goods first thing in the morning for shoes, which cost a dollar a pair, and proper . . . underpinnings."

He glares at Kathleen.

"Next week you'll get another blanket and aprons; your pay will be docked accordingly. Mrs. Treadwell is generous. Be grateful."

An extra blanket for the one bed we share! is the shout that nearly comes out of me, except that Kathleen stands on my toe.

She's been working the figures in her head. "Do you mean to say that you won't pay our agreed upon wage until the first Friday of July?" she says.

She's lightning with figures, my Kathleen. I'm still working it out on my fingers.

"You will take what I put in your hand, when I put it there, in the amount I choose, and be grateful. It's more than your kind deserves."

Reeve turns on his heel and swoops out the door like an old crow.

Kathleen paces the kitchen in fury. "The payment of an unjust wage is a sin. A sin!" she says to me.

I look at the trime in my hand—it's almost more insulting than getting nothing for all that toil.

Cook throws up her hands and abandons the dishes. "You Catholic girls and your just wages!"

She stomps over to the breadbox and shaves off a bit of cake thin as a holy wafer.

"You're all the same. Wailing about injustice. Did you know your Irish longshoremen have been on strike for higher wages? On strike! In the middle of a war! It's a disgrace."

She drizzles maple syrup over the top of the cake for good measure, puts two forks on the plate, and sets it on the table before me. It looks so sweet I could cry. I want it and I want nothing to do with these hard-hearted rich swells. I am grateful. And I'm furious. I want to go up to Reeve and punch him flat like Packy would. And I want to eat cake. It smells so good; I don't even know what it smells like, on account of I've never had cake before.

Cook shaves a wider slice for herself. "You Irish and your aid societies. Longshoremen's Union

Benevolent Society—there's the sound of trouble!"

She pours and even bigger dollop of syrup over her slice of cake.

"Friendly Sons of St. Patrick indeed," she grouses. "Doing for others what folk ought properly to be doing for themselves. You'll make us a nation of lazy Irishmen."

Cook sits down with a huge sigh. She slides a stool over and puts up her feet.

"It's the same tune everywhere you go. The lady of the house picks what her staff wears and takes the price of it from the wage. She'll be putting you in a new dress and apron for the soirée. See if she doesn't. It's all appearances with her. There's no point in fretting the butler. You'll get no sympathy there. Not a drop."

Cook shovels in forkfuls of cake. "Be reasonable, Bridget. This is a good situation. A thousand girls would kill for this job. A hundred will be on the doorstep tomorrow if you leave. Eat your cake. It's not so bad. You have a roof and a respectable position. Don't be so proud."

I surrender to the cake, burning with shame even as I shovel it in, one sweet forkful after another.

Kathleen sits like a stone. "She can make charge

against our wages at will? Are we to have no say in it?"

"Well, do you want your sister to have a coat this winter or no? You'll thank her for the clothing when the snow is falling. Don't think you won't. You'll be thanking her every night for that extra blanket, too."

Cook turns to me. She slides a card across the table with *Mrs. Elbridge J. Treadwell* written on it in curly letters. She points to it and then to me with her fork. "First thing in the morning you'll go down to Smith's Dry Goods. You'll go to the service door in the back, mind you." Cook punctuates this thought with vigorous waves of the fork. "Present the lady's card and they'll have your items. It's all arranged on credit. You'll bring them straight home. No dallying. No speaking to unsavory strangers."

I nod, eager for an excuse to get away from the laundry tubs.

"Then on Sunday morning, I want to see you both before church. Dressed properly. In the new shoes and underpinnings." She wags the fork over at Kathleen. "You'll walk to St. George's. And carry a polishing cloth with you because those new shoes had better be shining when you meet the lady's carriage there for nine o'clock services."

"Protestant services?" Kathleen says.

"If you know the prayers, you'll say them out properly or be silent."

Cook rabbits on, oblivious to Kathleen's shock. "If you know the songs, you'd better sing for the lady of the house. She'll like that. You know she will. You and your golden voice." Cook snorts in my general direction like a carthorse. "But don't drown out your betters. And for the love of God, girls, don't go spouting some vile papist nonsense. That will only get you in trouble. It's patriotic times now, what with the war. You don't want to go invoking foreign powers in public. Decent folk won't stand for it. All that kneeling down and lighting candles before graven idols. We don't hold with pagan practices in this house."

Kathleen gets redder with every slander Cook aims at the faith. I gulp down the last bite of cake and then tug her by the sleeve.

"Off to bed then," I say. "Lots to do tomorrow."

I get Kathleen safe into the stairwell before she boils over. All the way up the four flights she rails against the cook and the lady of the house and most of all lying Americans who say pretty words about freedom, but scratch off that crust of rights for the common man, and you're straight back to the high and mighty English and their bloody-handed ways.

When I finally close the door on our own room, Kathleen throws herself on the bed and wails. There is no consoling her. It's a sin to miss the Sunday Mass and it's a sin to worship against your conscience in a church not your own. And the lady of the house won't even let her go to confession to ease her soul.

I take our two coins and tie them up in our only handkerchief. I put them under a loose board in the floor. Our treasure is still in its bundle, still hidden away under the one bed. Still not saving us. I should unwrap it and demand answers, but Kathleen is so heart-scalded I can't make myself do it. I unbraid her hair nice and gentle and sing her to sleep.

MCCLELLAN'S CAMPAIGN

Preliminary Report of General McClellan of
the Battles of South Mountain and Antietam
Military Operations from the Time of the
Evacuation of Harrison's Landing Until Lee
was Driven Out of Maryland

—*New York Herald*

CHAPTER 9

SATURDAY, APRIL 4, 1863

Saturday morning I creep down the stairs before the house is awake, before the carts and wagons have kicked up the dust, before the milkman comes to the back door clattering his milk cans. I'm so sick of the skirt and the apron and the tiny world of kitchen and laundry. I spend all day on my feet, but I never go anywhere. Nothing to look at but the same rooms. No one to see but the same people. No wonder Cook and Sophia are sour to the core. It's a grand house, to be sure, but when you aren't allowed to read the books or even sit on the chairs, the shine goes off it in a hurry.

I snag a bun from the breadbox on my way out. None of the other washerwomen are about. It's dark in the shed, but the washtub is where I left it. I washed my old clothes on the sly yesterday.

I shuck off the dress, kick it into the corner, and pull on my britches. My own britches! The shirt goes on like a hug from the brothers. I give my back and shoulders a long stretch like a cat and then kick my legs up in the air just because I can. I peek out the shutters to the alley behind the yard. Not a soul stirring. Now's my chance.

"What are you after, little man?"

I freeze in my tracks. It's the washerwoman from next door, the one who told me to sing my way into this job. She's standing by her own washing shed, looking right at me.

She's got me on the spit now. If she tells the lady of the house, it's all over for Kathleen and me. She'll have a price for her silence though. Everybody does. I look her over in the dim light, wondering what she could want from me. We've worked side by side in separate yards for a week, and she's not said a word to me.

"Where are you going?" she says. "Are you running off and leaving that sister of yours?"

"No," I whisper. "Never!"

"Good," she says firmly. "You sister needs you; don't ever forget her."

She doesn't look greedy. She only looks weary.

"It'd be easier to forget a hurricane," I say cautiously.

"She's a Corker, to be sure," the woman says with a hint of pride. "She's all you need to see you through hard times. But you haven't answered my question."

"I haven't," I admit. "I was hoping you'd forget."

She folds her arms across her chest and waits.

Every now and then the truth works. I give it a go.

"We only lied so that we could stay together. But I'm so tired of pretending. I hate the feel of a skirt. The drag of it when you walk and the racket it makes when you move. Always catching on things. Underfoot on the stair. I hate walking slow and speaking soft. I hate all of it! Why is it so much work to be a girl?"

I didn't mean to say all of that. Didn't know it was in there. Now that it's out I hang my head. She reaches toward me, and I flinch in case she means to strike me, but she only cups my chin and raises my eyes to meet hers. She's not exactly smiling, but she's got a soft look.

"Just 'cause I'm good at lying doesn't mean I like it," I say.

"And why are you setting off into the city dressed in tatters?"

"The lady of the house sent me to get proper shoes and—things from the dry goods shop and . . . I just want to go as myself for once. I'll come back and take up the lie the minute I'm back, but out there"—I wave an arm at the city, a whole world of adventure away from the scrubbing and dusting— "I want to be myself out there."

"I remember my first week in service," the woman says. "We all do," she adds, nodding in the direction of the windows and wash yards all around us.

I've felt their stares all week, terrified of being discovered. Ashamed at all the times Cook has come out to scold me for my mistakes.

"I see you trying," she says. "Don't let those rich swells take the heart out of you."

I don't know what to say. Maybe Kathleen and I aren't so alone as we thought.

"I have a bargain in mind," she goes on. "Are you fast?"

"I'm the wind in a pair of shoes."

"Well, I've got a game leg and the walking to market every other day has me in agony. So here's my plan. Do my marketing and I'll get your morning wash up on the line so the ladies of your house won't miss you. If they see the wash up like it should be, they might not even notice you're gone."

I nod eagerly. Anything to get out of the scrubbing.

"There's one hitch though. You won't last a step in those clothes."

I look down at John's patched pants. I've been longing all week to pull Packy's jumper over my head and feel it like arms around me.

"Fresh off the boat," the woman says. "It won't matter if you carry the lady's calling card. The dry goods man will think you stole it and all your long walk will be for nothing."

I kick at the dirt.

"You've got to look like an American boy."

"There's no way I can pay for boy's clothes when all my wages are going to buy maid's things."

"I'll loan you a set of boy's clothes."

"You won't give us away?"

"Not on my life."

"I don't know where the market is."

"I'll draw a map. Can you read?"

"I can. My sister would see me dead before she'd let me skip on reading her whatever bit of the newspaper she can find. Even if it came to the house wrapped around a fish."

"You'll thank her for it one day."

"Probably. But I'll still smell like a fish when I do."

The woman chuckles and goes inside. She comes back with the most gorgeous suit of clothes—brown pants and a tan shirt, a thick checked jacket over that and as proper a cap as a boy ever had. I duck back into the shed to change. I'm an inch taller at least when I step out. I've never dressed so fine in all my life.

She looks me over with an approving nod. She hands me a paper with the list on one side and a map to Ryan's Grocery on the other.

"Tell them Eliza sent you." She gives me a red satchel to carry the groceries. "I'll need them by noon."

I head out of the alley at a dead run. I run for three blocks and then four into the foggy morning calm of a city not quite awake. I round the corner on block five, my old shoes singing over the street. I jump the streams of muck that run in the gutters. I dodge the milk wagon and the coal monger. It's not until I come across the iron gate of a cemetery that

I give thought to why Eliza has a set of boy's clothes to bargain with.

I stop running. I put a hand to the shirt as if I might feel the heart of the boy who wore it once. The gravestones stand like a regiment, each one casting a shadow on the pale grass. I don't believe in ghosts, but I cross myself anyway.

Walking now, I take in the sound of things. I hear languages I've never heard before, and smell breakfasts I couldn't name. Shopkeepers unlock their doors and workmen shoulder past each other, lunch buckets in hand. I come round a corner and there's an open block like a broken tooth among the buildings of Fifth Avenue. A half-built church rises out of the mud. White marble blocks are everywhere you look and the beginnings of three arched doorways face the street. Rough-handed men pour onto the site. A pair of them in homespun caps are from Galway, by the sound of it. I can hear my Da in their talk. I nearly weep to hear them; I miss the men of the house. I'm all that's left and I'm shut away in a house full of women.

The men fall to work. Each one has a place— mixing mortar in a barrow, laying out rollers to move the great blocks of marble, line haulers, blade grinders. Off to the side there's an old man cloaked in dust calling the martyrs and saints out of stone with nothing but a mallet and a chisel.

A group of workers comes to move the stone block beside me. "Keep clear of the lifting rigs," one of them says to me. He's a Galway man for sure.

"Nice and easy," another man says as they lay rollers in front of the block. A barrel-chested man with a pry bar works the block onto the rollers. Two more burly fellows put their shoulders to the block to move it along. One of the men calls out the working rhythm.

"*Eins, und, zwei, und . . .*"

The block rolls into position, and the Irishman who spoke to me makes a rope harness for the block and ties it fast to the lifting rig. Another fellow strides up to check the knots.

"All right, men," he says. "Pull together now!"

The men take one end of the line.

"Heave. Ho. Heave. Ho."

The men fall into a working rhythm. The block rises by inches.

"Put your back into it!" the foreman shouts.

It's an agony of work to raise the marble block an inch. And they've got to lift it up to a wall that is already tall as a tree.

"Ya wee slackers," the foreman taunts. "Are ya nothing but a bunch of girls in skirts? Pull now!"

He has no idea how hard a girl in a skirt works.

I know a good hauling tune. I stand up on my stone block and sing out "The Boys of Blue Hill."

"*Da, da, dum, da-diddly-dum.*" It's Packy's favorite tune, a hornpipe with a good swing for working-men to pull a rope to. "*Bup, bup, dum, bup-iddly-um.*" I sing out the tune and the workers pull in a bigger breath and dig a little deeper. The stone rises above my head and then higher. I keep singing, straining to be heard over the city noises.

I can hear my Packy calling out the step he taught me. "Tip down tip down. Shuffle hop back." I don't want to dance. Not without him. But them devils in my shoes give me no peace. I try a shuffle step. I like how the nail I put in the left shoe to hold it together another year clicks on the marble. I close my eyes to the builders and think of home.

Tip down tip down. Shuffle-hop-back. Bang, click, shuffle-hop-back.

"Shoulders back," Packy would say to me. "Like you're looking for a fight."

I haven't danced this hornpipe in a year. Not since Packy's wake. But the tune has hold of me now and won't let go. The hornpipe he taught me lives in my legs even when my head doesn't want to remember. I make the lead-around a tight circle on my block of marble and launch into the second step.

"Straight and tall," my Da would say to me.

Leap over. Click. Shuffle-step. Bang. Click. Shuffle-step.

By the time my hornpipe is done, they've pulled the rope as far as it will go and the men on top of the wall are sliding the stone into place. I've danced a block of marble a mile in the air. Take that, Packy! You haven't done more yourself.

"Be gone with you!" the foreman shouts at me. "'Tain't a schoolyard here."

I hop off the block and scurry away to glad shouts of farewell from my Galway men. I've got a smile on my face as I go. A hundred years from now, I'm going to point at that stone in the whole grand church and say, *There's the block I danced into place.*

CHAPTER 10

SATURDAY, APRIL 4, 1863

I'm still smiling a dozen blocks later when I come to Smith's Dry Goods. I steer clear of the fancy front doors and go around back. The man at the storeroom has shelves floor to ceiling full of uniforms. I hand him Mrs. Treadwell's card. He gets out shoes, bloomers, undershirts, aprons, caps, and hallelujah! Socks. He wraps it up in paper and ties the bundle with twine.

Back on the street, I take a look at Eliza's map.

"Lost?"

A man with a gray beard and spectacles sits in his tailor shop at a treadle sewing machine. He has a kind look. A black man with a carpenter's tool belt stands outside mending his broken window.

"I'm after Ryan's Grocery on Sixth Avenue I say. "And then Sullivan's butcher shop."

"You're not far at all," the tailor says. "Three blocks on and it will be on the right side of the street."

"Sullivan's is four blocks farther," the carpenter adds. "Across from the park."

I get a stab of sorrow to see the tools hanging from his belt—the square and hammer. Da had those tools and they would have been mine someday.

"Thank you." Neither of these fellows are Irish but they don't show a lick of scorn for my freckles or my accent. Maybe Americans aren't so alike after all. "Thank you kindly," I say and they wave me on my way.

The greengrocer's is a marvel. Bins upon bins of vegetables: potatoes and rhubarb, peas and greens, asparagus and spinach, onions and apples. I've never seen the choices. I'm so enchanted I don't see Mr. Ryan himself, but he must have seen Eliza's red satchel because he calls out from behind me.

"Michael! Are ye back from the wars?" He claps a hand on my shoulder.

I don't know what to say. I turn around slow. "I'm Eliza's neighbor. Doing her marketing for a favor."

The grocer heaves a heavy sigh. "Poor Michael," he says. "I haven't heard from my Jackie either. Not for weeks on end."

I squirm in my shoes. "Are they drummers?" I ask, remembering the recruiter at dockside.

"Jackie started out a drummer, but he's a great lad of fourteen. They'll be giving him a gun any day now."

"You can be a soldier at fourteen?"

In the portrait in Mrs. Treadwell's parlor, Valor has a gun, but he's eighteen at least; he must be. Mrs. Treadwell was going on to her friend Mrs. Vanderzanden about what a marksman he is. She bought him a sword besides the gun because it looked dashing on him. As if the whole war were a stage play done up for her pleasure.

"Such losses our lads have seen," the grocer goes on. "Half the Brigade buried in the bloody lanes of Antietam. Five hundred more in the frozen ground at Fredericksburg."

"Five hundred?" I feel a dead weight in the pit of my stomach. There aren't five hundred people in my hometown. We came to America to stop fighting—to stop dying. How can we still be fighting when the English aren't even here?

"There was a man by the docks that asked me to join the Irish Brigade. He said he'd pay me. There was a contract and all. Do they really pay a fellow when he fights?"

"Don't get caught up in talk of glory, lad. Stay close to your Ma. Give her comfort while ye can."

The memory of my mother flares up in me like a struck match. I hand over the list and turn away so I don't shame myself. He fills Eliza's satchel with carrots and leeks and potatoes and herbs. I form a new notion of my fellow washerwoman and her silences.

I head back at a walk now, savoring the freedom to take a stride as long as I like and sit with my knees apart when I rest. I walk past the Colored Orphan Asylum and five blocks farther on a somber building set back from the street that says Columbia College on the gate. Wouldn't Kathleen love that! I savor a picture of her taking a seat among the scholars, correcting the spelling and manners of the lot of them. I confess I love the idea of her being a teacher mostly because she'll have somebody else to command.

One more stop for sausages and the satchel is full

to bursting and the smell of the meat only teasing me and not a torture, now that I know there'll be food in my own bowl tonight. What a difference a week makes. I'm every bit as lean and bony as I was before, but I can work through a whole day without falling asleep. I can't remember the last time that's happened.

I keep walking through crowds of folk up to the big park. In all these thousands, there's none that know me. Ever since we got our job, I've been longing to tell someone, "We made it! We're still alive." But nobody is waiting for a letter.

The park is a mix of grass and trees and mud. There are half-built bridges over paths that have been marked out but not paved. The big open field has soldiers and their tents at one end, a parade ground in the middle, and shanties on the other side. The shanties are cobbled together with loose boards and stones and shingles and canvas. Some have men lying sick and weary on the ground. Others have families and lines of washing and even a few chickens or a pig in a pen. I hear mostly Irish voices and a little bit of German. Porridge bubbles in a pot over an open fire. The drafty room I share with Kathleen in the attic is a palace compared to this.

From the edge of the park I hear a new sound. A tune I know, but played on something I've never heard before. I follow my ears to the park gate on Sixtieth Street. There's a man in a muddy blue uniform and soldier's cap, sitting on a bucket, playing a tune. It sounds halfway between a pennywhistle and an accordion, but it's a little thing he's got hidden in his hand. He slides it up and down his mouth to puff out a tune.

I can't stop watching the man. He's a weatherworn fellow with a bandage around his gray head and a stump where a foot should be, but he's playing an upbeat jig tune like he hasn't a care in the world. He's not even looking around to make sure he doesn't get caught. Folks stream past him but some stop and listen, and every once in a while they drop a coin in his tin cup.

I see a copper coming and duck into the bushes. The copper walks straight past the man without beating him with the nightstick or taking his money. It's a marvel! I believe that man could take the money straight home with him after.

"God bless you," folks murmur as they give him a coin. The old soldier never looks up but goes on playing one jaunty tune after another. He starts up

"The Arkansas Traveler," which I heard the sailors singing on the boat. It's a catchy one. I can't help singing out loud.

Oh, 'twas down in the woods of the Arkansas,
And the night was cloudy and the wind was raw . . .

It's a rouser. Pretty soon a person stops and then another. Toes are a-tapping through the chorus and the old soldier shows no sign of stopping. He even throws in a flourish or two for style. I'm about to sing it again when somebody in the back calls out, "Jig it, laddie."

Who can resist that? Not me. Not for a minute. I bang out a treble reel, the best I got. When it's done there's a little rain of pennies in the old soldier's cup and three different fellows come up to me and press a coin in my hand.

I run home floating a foot above the ground. I sneak down the alley and change back into the maid's dress. I hate it, but as I fold up the pants and shirt Eliza loaned me, I think about all those wretches living in shacks in the park. Those cold hungry streets are out there, waiting to swallow Kathleen and me up. If dressing as a girl keeps us from living in squalor, it's not the worst bargain.

Eliza is working at her washtub. My morning's stack of clothes is up on the line and she's hanging up her own. I head over to Eliza's yard with her satchel. If I was still wearing pants, I'd jump the fence but now I have to go out my back gate and in hers.

"Your marketing," I say to her. I cut my eyes right and left to check for eavesdroppers. "And thank you," I whisper.

"Well then—Mary is it?" Eliza says, taking the satchel full of groceries.

"It is."

It's a sin to hate the Blessed Mother's name. I know it is. I should be proud of it. I should be meek and good. But pretending is as far as I'll go. Inside, I'm the black-hearted sinner that hates being called Mary, every single time.

"If you ever had a brother, Mary, what do you suppose you'd call him?"

My heart skips a beat. She has something on me now. She could tell and I'd be finished.

But she did the washing for me in fair trade for the groceries. And she has a boy of her own to fit the clothes she loaned me. Somewhere on a battlefield is her Michael, a boy who was once just my size.

"Well, Patrick's a good name," I say.

"Oh, indeed."

"I'd call him Packy, of course. Christy's not a bad name either."

"For St. Christopher. The patron of travelers would be good name for any brother of yours."

"John's a fine name for a boy."

"Goodness, how many brothers do you plan to have?" She's smiling now. "A girl would be lucky to have so many." She picks up a dishtowel and pins it to the line. "She'd be lucky to even have one." That cost her to say. I can feel it, and her with the one boy so far from her on the field of battle.

"Daniel!" I say. "I'd call him Daniel."

"After the Great Emancipator, Daniel O'Connell himself? There's a freedom fighter for the ages."

"He is." I straighten my shoulders like any boy proud of his heritage would do and then I remember the way a girl should stand.

Even as I slide my shoulders down and forward, Eliza says, "It's a name to live up to. Is it not?" Before I can think of a safe thing to say, she goes on. "Daniel O'Connell had a golden voice too—a voice to move multitudes. Music must run in your family."

"It did."

We all used to sing and dance. Da had a penny-whistle he kept hidden in his sleeve. He'd play a tune and make me sing it back to him, but he never taught me to play. And when the police came round to make trouble, they always wrote him down as Patrick the carpenter or Patrick the farmer. Never Patrick the musician.

"But the sweet voice you have now won't last, and you won't be able to hide when it goes," Eliza says. "I won't betray you, Daniel. But in time your own voice will."

A knot forms up inside me. I remember the changing of the voice for my brothers. It comes on you sudden and you'd sooner hold back the tide than stop it. Before I can answer Eliza, Kathleen comes storming across the yard.

"Mary, God help us, I will skin you alive and fry you in butter. The whole house is calling for you! Where have you been? The music master will be here at noon and you have to be dressed fit to meet him."

She's about to grab me by the ear and drag me over the fence, so I drop one of them pretty curtseys she makes me practice and I sing out "I'm coming!" in the most girlish tone I can manage. She keeps her pinching fingers to herself. There are a few tiny advantages to being a girl and I'm claiming every one of them.

Kathleen hustles me up the stairs with such a torrent of scoldings that I decide, purely for spite, not to tell her about the money I got from dancing and keep it for myself. She'd only plague me for changing out of my disguise.

At the top, the lady of the house sweeps me into one of the bedrooms that's been closed up to now. I can see by the lack of ribbons and lace and by the collection of snail shells on the windowsill and the baseball bat in the corner that it must be Valor's room.

"Don't touch anything," Mrs. Treadwell says sternly. She points to the pale blue dress Sophia has laid out for me. It's full of ruffles and beads and bother. It must be something Temperance wore years ago.

I shoot a panicked look at Kathleen. The women of the house, I've learned, dress in a room all together. The lady's maid helps with lacing and buttoning. They put on jewels and rings and ribbons and clasps, and the whole time they cluck away at each other like so many chickens in a coop.

What if she wants to fuss over me? The lady of

the house takes to fussing over dresses like a drunk takes to the pub. The dread of her walking in where she pleases fills me with terror every time I use the privy. I can't even stand up like a proper man in there. I have to squat like a dog, just in case she opens the door.

"Let me help her with the buttoning up," Kathleen says. She comes in and closes the door, shutting Mrs. Treadwell out.

"I can't wear this. It's too fancy," I whisper to her.

"You'll do as the lady pleases." Kathleen starts in on the silk buttons while I open the parcel from the shop and get out the aprons and underpinnings.

"Oh thank God," Kathleen says and snatches up the larger of the bloomers. She turns her back to me and slips them right on under her dress. I don't like the look of them, not one bit. But a boy has to eat. I slip mine on and tug off the black uniform.

Kathleen drops a slip over my head, wraps me in a belly squeezer, and then drops a petticoat over that. Finally the shiny blue dress slides over my head. She buttons me up the back. It's as smooth as glass to the touch but I feel like an onion in all these layers. I don't know how I'll draw a breath, let alone sing.

"Oh, Danny," Kathleen says when I turn around. She sighs—actually sighs with delight. "Look at you."

"I will not."

"You're a picture."

I could spit!

"They'll never guess, Danny. Never. You are just so . . . pretty. I'm sorry. I know you hate this." She gives me a quick hug and then holds me at arm's length to inspect my disguise.

I scowl while she fluffs up my curls.

"I'll be due a medal for valor before we're done." I grit my teeth while she places a bow in my hair.

Kathleen sighs again and takes my two hands in hers. "Listen to me now. You hold your head up in that music room. Don't ever—"

The lady of the house busts in without knocking, blue satin slippers in hand and all a-flap about the fit of the dress. She squirts toilette water on me because for some reason she thinks smelling like an orange peel is important to a good music lesson. She fusses over that bow in my hair. I trade in my usual growl for a girlish sigh and bear it with the patience of a martyr. Before, I was nervous to meet the music master, but now I'll take any reason at all to get away from the lady of the house.

She takes me by the arm and steers me down the wide front staircase like I'm a real member of the household while Kathleen scurries down the servant's stairs in pitch darkness. She emerges just in time to see me turn into the music room—a parlor so fancy only Sophia is allowed to dust it.

Temperance is already dressed for the occasion and has arranged herself on the piano bench. She glances earnestly at the pages of music. I look at my toes and then the walls and then the ceiling with equal earnestness.

A man comes puffing up the marble stairs after Reeve with a sheaf of papers under one arm and a baton in hand. He is as round and ruddy as Reeve is pale and lean.

"Good afternoon, Mrs. Treadwell," he says at the door, still slightly out of breath from the stairs. "I hope you are well."

He sweeps into the room and goes immediately to the vase of flowers that drops all the annoying petals and pollen that I have to sweep up twice a day. "Lilacs! Beautiful!" he takes a deep appreciative sniff. "My dear Mrs. Treadwell, how is your son? What do you hear from the fields of glory?"

"He's fine," Mrs Treadwell says with a brittle

smile. "He's glorious, in fact. A credit to his unit." She fusses with the flowers spilling even more pollen on the furniture that was just polished to a gloss that would put a still pond to shame. I fight the urge to scoot over there and wipe it up.

Temperance looks at her mother with thinly disguised shock. There hasn't been a letter from Valor, not one. Cook frets about him after she's had a cup or two of the wet. Plain to see he was her favorite, too.

Mrs. Treadwell shoots Temperance a warning look while the maestro is absorbed in admiring the paintings. When he is done she hops up from the piano, makes her curtsey, and says, "Good afternoon, Maestro." I copy her. The lady of the house clamps an arm firmly around my shoulder.

"May I present our Mary," she beams with pride. "Beloved daughter of a dear friend not quite as fortunate as I," she goes on in a confiding tone. "A rare talent—I couldn't help myself, I just had to make the sacrifice of taking her in and treating her as my own." She runs a chilly fingernail down the side of my face. "I just know she'll be a famous singer one day. We must do all we can for the jewels of talent that come our way. Any true artist would do the same."

I could push that true artist right out the window and not feel a moment of regret.

The maestro is all flattery. "A jewel for the polishing," he says warmly. "Fear not, madam, she will bloom in my care." He smiles and lifts the baton. "Let's warm up with a C scale. Andante, if you please." He looks at me expectantly.

He lost me back at C scale. All that comes to mind are fish scales, and then cod obviously, because it's the only fish I can think of that begins with C, and then of course I'm straight to imagining fish in a pan sizzling in a pat of butter.

"Dear me," the maestro says, still holding the baton, but now looking perplexed.

I have no idea what he's asking me to do. I start to sweat. Temperance smirks as I squirm, but then Maestro waves the baton in her direction, and she plunks on the keys all in a row. Is that it? He could have said *walk your voice up the stair* and saved us the trouble. I sing out the same notes.

"There we go!" Maestro says. "A natural ear."

Maybe this will be easy.

We sing a dozen more not-fish scales and then move on to something Maestro calls arpeggios, which is like skipping a stone over the scale. I thought

I'd mind the lesson—being book-learned a piece of music rather than catching it, like a bird in the open—but I don't. The music master is demanding. He stops me and makes me repeat where I've gone wrong. But he makes Temperance do the same, so that's fair.

I thought I'd mind singing in Italian, too, but it's not so bad once you latch onto the rhythm of it. It's all long oohs and aahs, and you'd never gather a crowd at a crossroads with the aria he wants me to sing, but the tune is sweet and airy like a feather in the wind.

Written-down music is the real revelation. It's nothing but a crowd of dots perched on a fence, but when you get the hang of how they work, I reckon any tune at all could be put down for good and last in this world in a way singers don't. In the whole house full of one grand thing after another, the only bit of it I want to steal is the blank pages in Temperance's music book. What I wouldn't pour out onto those pages.

Temperance doesn't know any songs by heart. She doesn't have to remember. She doesn't wake up in the middle of the night with her father's favorite tune rolling around in her head and the last phrase of it locked away in a box you can never open.

No. She'll never know what it means for her own music to be a crime. She can play that piano any time she likes, loud as it pleases her, and even with the windows open if she chooses.

I know it's a sin to covet what somebody else has, but I want those blank music pages and I'd steal them if I wasn't afraid.

SANITARY REFORMS

Six thousand families in New York live in underground cellars without air, without light—undrained receptacles of stagnant water in which decent cleanliness is nearly impossible and tolerable health nearly so . . .

—*New York Daily Tribune*

CHAPTER 11

WEDNESDAY, MAY 6, 1863

Weeks pass and I resist stealing the sheets of music, but I just can't stop dressing as myself and running free in the city to do Eliza's marketing and to dance for tips. Not that I've breathed a word of it to the great tyrant Kathleen. No, I've been keeping it to myself, mostly to prevent my own murder. She's always hissing at me for any hint of boyishness. She'd have an apoplexy if she knew I was going out in my right clothes. Better she doesn't know.

I take a secret satisfaction in my growing stash of coins and come to dread the way the rain cuts into my audience. Maybe someday I'll have enough to leave the Treadwells and get a place of our own. Boys my own age, younger even, sell newspapers in the street. It looks like better work than bending over washtubs in a dress all day long, but newsboys are out in all weather. They sleep rough, and for sure they don't eat as well as me—three plates a day and cake when it strikes Cook's mood to give me some. I won't do it. I'd die of shame to bring Kathleen out on to the streets after all we've been through.

One morning in May on my way to Ryan's grocery, Matteo the barber calls out to me from his corner shop. His door is flung wide. The smell of soap and wisps of cut hair drift into the street.

"*Ragazzo!*" he shouts. "Show us a step!" Matteo is a lover of music, always singing at work. His voice is so deep and grand I get a shiver of joy when I hear him. I give him a skip-two-three and then my best leap—the one where I click my heels twice before I land.

"Ta da!" I shout, bowing grandly to the waiting men in the barbershop, who give me a hearty cheer—though the half-shaved fellow in the chair looks none too pleased. Matteo sets down his blade and fishes a licorice drop out of his jar.

"Come now," he says, handing over the candy and picking up a scissor. "Let's give you a trim."

I shake my head and take a step back. Mrs. Treadwell would whip me, and maybe Kathleen, too, if I cut off the curls that she so loves to see done up in ribbons. I could take it. I would. But if that woman lays a hand on my Kathleen . . . well, I'd do something not girlish for certain. Matteo ignores my dismay. He's in performance mode now. He waves the scissor over his head.

"La la la." Snip snip. "La la la." Snip snip. "For you, *ragazzo,* I will do it for a song!" The men in the shop laugh and egg him on, though not so much the fellow in the barber chair.

I recognize the tune from Temperance's piano lesson. I sing the next line of the tune back to him, a whole octave up. I'm a verse into it when I remember that the maestro said this is a love song. So I make a pantomime of a grand lady singing opera and falling in love with herself in the mirror. I get the whole shop roaring—well, except for the one fellow with a face full of lather.

"*Bellissimo,*" Matteo says, returning at last to shaving his customer. "You should sing for Big Al. He's starting up a variety show. Finest stage in the Bowery."

Wouldn't that be grand! I take a moment to savor the thought of dancing on a real stage instead of a street corner. Kathleen would roast me on a spit just for thinking of it. With a sigh and a wave I'm on my way.

Talk of war is everywhere. At Ryan's grocery the customers are fretting over the one paper with the headline about troops gathering for a battle at Chancellorsville. Two women at the butcher shop are arguing about another newspaper laying blame for the humiliating loss at Antietam. The paper Kathleen read to me last week listed off the number of freed slaves that are going to swarm north and take all the jobs in the factories and on the docks. The one I read to her yesterday swore the freed slaves would all be sent west to work in timber and mining. At home there was just the one paper that favored the English and the one that favored the Irish. A person knew where he stood with the news.

Daniel O'Connell, himself spoke against slavery. He was eloquent on the topic—everyone says so. This Frederick Douglass fellow who writes a newspaper, he came to Ireland and met with O'Connell. Mr. Douglass spoke his praises afterward. But what would O'Connell have thought of us now? Should we fight for another man's freedom? I think he'd say yes. I want to live right. But I want to live, too.

I see the same old soldier on Sixtieth Street at the edge of the park most every week. I look for him, if I'm honest. We've formed what you'd call a silent partnership on account of he never speaks. He plays the mouth organ and once in a while he breaks out a pair of spoons and beats time with them between his hand and knee. There's a lot more music than you'd think in a spoon. I'm itching to try it out but there's no way playing the spoons is a girlish thing to do. Beside which, Cook would slice off my arms with a cleaver if she caught me messing about with the cutlery. She doesn't hold with music and snorts in disgust every time the lady of the house calls me away for a music lesson.

This morning I see a bootblack working near where I usually sing and dance. He has a wooden box and all manner of rags draped over his shoulder. He's brown as a fiddle, and he's whistling a tune and slapping a beat on the shine box. The old soldier is nowhere in sight but I wait for him, tapping a toe in time to the bootblack's rhythm.

A dandy in a top hat and tailcoat walks up to him, and the man jumps to his feet. "Shine your shoes, sir?" He slides the box into position.

The dandy puts his foot on the box and the bootblack kneels in front of him. He uses a rough cloth and a sharp stick to pick all the mud and manure off the man's shoes. He whistles as he works and the tune casts a spell over me. I give myself over to learning it, humming under my breath and swaying to get a feel for the tempo of it. The bootblack takes a cake of polish and rubs it on his rag. He spreads the polish over the shoe and then, uses a long smooth cloth, to buff up a shine. All the while he keeps whistling that tune.

It's not a reel. It's not a jig either and for a minute I think it's some kind of new hornpipe because it's got a bit of a swing in the rhythm. I try out a few shuffle-hop-bangs to see if they fit but they don't. It's such a good tune, I can't resist trying.

The man puts up his other shoe and the bootblack goes back to the beginning of his song. This time through, I see how the rhythm of the tune fits the rhythm of how he slides the polish on a shoe. I switch to shuffle-hop-slide and it fits.

I'm so thrilled to feel my dance come together that I toss in a spin at the end of the phrase. Folks stop to watch, so I add the clicky heels trick that's such a crowd-pleaser.

The dandy bobs his head along to the beat and when his shoes shine like a prize mare, he steps off the box. He takes a nickel and drops it on the pavement.

"Thank you, sir." The bootblack bends to retrieve the coin.

"Fine bit of footwork," the dandy says to me. He presses a penny in my hand and walks off.

As soon as he's gone the bootblack stands up. He's a lot taller than me. His clothes were nice once but they've seen wear. He gives me a good shove.

"Who do you think you are, stealing a man's work place? Ain't it enough you Irish have stolen all our jobs?"

I stagger back a few steps. It's wrong to take a man's work place. It's like breaking a strike. Da would be ashamed of me if ever I did it; all my brothers would.

"I'm sorry. I'm new here."

"You're all new here, ship rat! Go find your own job and dance to your own music."

"I didn't mean you harm." I hold out my penny to him but he won't take it. Maybe I should throw it on the ground beside him like the other gentleman did, but it feels rude to me and Ma would be horrified if I turned out to be as rude as a gentleman. It's right up there among the sins, alongside being drunk as a lord.

"Please take it," I say. I don't know what else to do.

"I don't want your money, you little hopping canary," he says. "And I don't need your charity. I need to work, in peace, the same as any man."

A gentlemen steps out of the cab that has been standing on the sidewalk. He's got black whiskers, a pearl-handled cane and a weary look. He's a lot dirtier than a man with his cut of tie usually is— not a dandy at all. He's got the weathered look of a workingman.

"Well, here's a sad state of things," the man says. "Two musicians fighting."

I look at the ground and pull my cap low, even more ashamed of myself.

"Here's a penny each, since the whistling was as fine as the dancing." He holds out a penny to me and sets one on the box for the bootblack.

"Thank you," I say.

"I'd like a shine, boy," the man with the cane says.

The bootblack hops to it and I start to edge away.

"There's no shame in honest work," the man says. "I wasn't always rich."

The bootblack goes on polishing as if the man is not talking at all.

"No shame at all in working your way up from the bottom of the pile. I've done worse than shine shoes in my day. Or dance on the street for pennies," he adds, turning to me.

I should keep my mouth shut. I should just melt into the crowd and go away, but something the bootblack said really chafes me.

"Is it true?" I blurt out. "Are the Irish taking jobs from black men?"

"It's true," the man says. "You Irish who swarmed in twenty years ago would do the work for less than we used to pay black carpenters and smiths and hod carriers and ditch diggers. And that's bad news for every working man, no matter what his color, for now we pay all of you less than your labor is worth."

The bootblack makes a gruff noise in his throat, which could mean *That's right*, or it could mean, *Neither of you knows a thing you're talking about.*

The cut of his shirt is as good as the man whose shoes he is polishing. Except for the silk tie and the color of their skin they could be the same man. How did the bootblack come to be the one kneeling on the pavement and tending another man's shoes? He wasn't always poor.

I don't want this man's troubles to be the fault of my countrymen. If anyone should have a care for folk who are treated ill—treated ill for the thing about themselves they can't change—it would be the Irish. But the newspapers say all different things and there's no Ma or Da or even a parish priest to ask what's the truth of the matter.

I take a breath and keep trying. "But the newspapers say it's the freed slaves that are all going to come up here and take jobs from the rest of us. The newspapers say the war is their fault."

"You shouldn't be reading newspapers at your age," the man says. "Not a scrap of truth in them!"

"There's nothing else to read."

"Hmph!" the man says. "You ever hear of a public library?"

"I haven't."

"Well, you should!"

I ought to say '*yes, sir*'. Cook always says '*yes, ma'am*', no matter what outrageous thing the woman of the house says. *Yes* is such an abrupt word, such an English word, I never use it and now it's too late. The gentleman starts rattling on and I'm stuck listening.

"You Irish think you're so wise because you can read. You're only as smart as the reading you choose," he says. "Those newspapermen can fashion a chain of words and lead you around with them as sure as any slave in irons. And you're the greater fool, thinking you're better than a slave. At least a slave sees the chain that's leading him."

I don't know what to think. I don't want slaves to suffer. I don't want free black folk to suffer. But *I* don't want to suffer either. We can't all win.

The bootblack finishes the shine. The man with the pearl-handled cane sets his nickel on the box and walks away. I walk away too, thinking I've wronged a neighbor far more than just dancing in his work place, and I don't know how to make amends.

★★★

Back at the Treadwell house Kathleen wedges me into the music lesson dress again. The lady of the house has added extra lessons to torture her daughter, who doesn't even like to play in front of people. I don't mind the singing, but I've come to loathe that dress. I break out in itches at the mere thought of it and the play-acting that goes along.

The speed at which Mrs. Treadwell can switch from excoriating me for some little fault in my sweeping and dusting, to acting like I'm her prized heifer for show at the county fair, makes my head spin. Still, there's a safety of sorts in the charade and I play along for Kathleen's sake. Every time she hears the maestro praise my singing she puffs up like a chicken strutting the coop.

The whole place is a humming hive of preparations. Music and poetry are meat and air for the lady of the house. She's thrown her whole self into the spectacle she's planning. Invitations in grand curly writing went out last week. July thirteenth is only ten weeks away. Gowns and new draperies were ordered. Cook has been searching for just the right dish, only to have the lady of the house change her mind because missus so-and-so served the same thing at a party so grand Mrs. Treadwell and even Mrs. Vanderzanden weren't invited.

I've already learned the first aria the maestro planned for me and he's started me in on another. Kathleen gave me an earful about not showing up the lady's daughter for the average musician she is. Her mother has set her mind that the society women will be so taken with Temperance's musical skill, they will invite the daughter to all the swanky balls she doesn't get invited to herself.

In Ireland if the lord and lady of the house don't like your da, they don't like you either. I don't know why it would be different here.

Temperance is a flood of tears on account of her mother's wild ambitions. She doesn't want a husband. Fair play to her. Kathleen doesn't want one either. The lady of the house has her mind made up, though, so I don't see how she'll escape a trip up the middle aisle.

But I do see the danger in making the daughter of the house look bad, especially with the mother sitting in the corner at every music lesson, watching like a crow watches a battlefield. I resolve to learn the next aria slowly. I'm off to a convincing start—a dash off-pitch and completely dodgy on the tempo.

We haven't gotten ten measures into the song when Reeve barges in. Mrs. Treadwell dismisses him with a wave of her hand.

He doesn't go.

"Reeve?"

"Mr. Treadwell has sent a letter, ma'am." He holds out a silver tray with the post.

"Really, Reeve! Music over mail, if you please."

"I took note of the return address, ma'am."

The lady of the house snatches the letter off his tray and slits it with a hairpin. She paces the parlor and reads the paper over twice with increasing agitation.

"Excuse me, Maestro," she says with forced calm. "We must cut our lesson short today. Thank you."

"As you wish, madam," he says with a courteous bow. He gestures toward the sheet music on the piano. "Careful attention to the tempo, my dears, and we will take this up next week."

As soon as the front door closes behind him, the lady of the house throws open the parlor door.

"Reeve! Cook! Sophia! Bridget!" she bellows.

The staff comes a-running, Kathleen at the end of the line, bewildered as the rest of them.

"Mr. Treadwell is coming home. He will be here this evening."

Everyone falls into a flurry of activity, each servant to her own task. Temperance hops up from the piano and hurries to her room. Kathleen and I stand dumbfounded.

"Go do something with that girl," the lady of the house says to Kathleen. "Make her presentable."

Kathleen bobs a curtsey and dashes upstairs.

"Clean sheets!" she barks at me.

I scamper off to change out of my music practice clothes and then strip the beds, hoping that cook has water hot and that the day is warm enough to dry them. If not, Mr. Treadwell will be sleeping on damp sheets.

Once I'm out of the fancy dress and back in the plain, I scoot down the hall to collect the sheets for the laundry. The door to Temperance's room is ajar so I peek inside.

There's a wreck of fancy dresses strewn across the bed where there's usually only books. Kathleen has the young lady in a chair and is smoothing her hair into a crown of braids.

"Do you think this dress suits me?"

Temperance and her mirror are not friends. By the blotches on her face I'd say she's been crying.

"It's fine, Miss," Kathleen says. "An excellent shade of blue."

"Oh, how were you and I cursed with brown hair?" Temperance says. "Everyone favors the blonde. You see how Mother dotes on your sister. She was just the same with Valor. It isn't fair!"

"The Blessed Mother had brown hair," Kathleen says soothingly. "And she is exalted above all women."

"If only I were a brilliant poet like Mr. Whitman!" Temperance snatches a book from her dressing table. "Then no one would care how I look."

Kathleen glances at the open page. "If you were a man and sixty years old, I imagine you could go about looking like a haystack in a wrinkled suit whether you were a poet or no."

"Bridget! The things you say." A smirk begins to break out.

"The picture doesn't show it but he's got a mouse in his pocket. I'll wager money."

"Surely not."

"And this time of year he can be found with a wren nesting in his beard."

Temperance finally lets loose with a giggle. It's a relief to see Kathleen breaking through her shell. It's not enough to do the work you're asked—the women of the house have to *like* us if we're going to be safe. Mrs. Treadwell doesn't love me but she loves my voice and that keeps me out of the weather, but Kathleen has to find her own way into the cramped heart of her mistress.

I go down the hall, gather up the sheets, and grope my way down the dark stairway, arms overflowing with laundry. One false step and I'll tumble end over end like the one maid I heard tell of who fell down the stair and never walked again after. Our whole lives here hang in a fearful balance.

Last week a Bridget down the street was sent away for kissing the knife grinder. Eliza said it wasn't even true. The woman of the house took a dislike to the girl and made up an excuse to dismiss her. Weeping in the alley she was. The other maids and cooks on the block came out to their back fences with a coin or a bit from the kitchen or the name of folk who might take her in. After she left, their talk took a dark turn.

"She's done for," said Alice from across the alley.

"Sleeping rough in the park before the week's out I shouldn't wonder," said Ann.

"Poor lamb," said Jane, who cooks in the same house with Ann. "Alone in the world. No one left to take her in."

"It'll serve her right, the shameless hussy. We all look bad when one of us strays," Alice said. All the women and girls nodded sadly from their back fences. "They already don't like it when I go walking out on a Sunday with my intended. Sure the wedding's in a month and they can't bear the sight of the man for the one hour a week I spend in his company."

"Hard enough to find a man already," said the Bridget whose name really is Bridget. "And us so far from them down in the Five Points and missing all the frivolity—the Friday night firehouse suppers, the ceili dances at the corner shop on a Saturday night." She sighed and cast an eye downtown.

"Marriage isn't everything," Ann said briskly. "Who needs a man? You've got a roof against the rain and food enough to keep body and soul together."

"And we've got each other for company," Jane added. "I'll take your sweet faces over anything grizzled and grouchy I'd find at one of your firehouse suppers."

Eliza laughed and so did Ann, but Alice was having none of it. "She'll end a ruin, mark my words."

"Never you mind, Mary," Eliza said to me, shooing me back to work. "She'll land on her feet, so she will. Plenty of work for a clever girl like her."

"If she keeps clear of the dance saloons," Cook said grimly. She yanked the new peas off their stems and tossed them in her basket. "Music," she snorted in distain. "Root of all evil." She gathered up her greens and grumbled all the way to the kitchen door.

"Not her," said Ann. "She'd never."

"Surely not the dance saloons," Bridget chimed in. The others nodded and murmured in agreement. I saw them twisting their handkerchiefs into worry knots or crossing themselves and lifting up silent prayers for safety. And then they all scurried back to their mistresses, smiles pasted on over their fears.

I put all of that out of my mind. They'll never catch me kissing anyone—for sure not the knife grinder. Even so, I grate soap into the washtub and pour in water from the stove. I put my heart and soul into scrubbing the sheets to make up a fine bed for the man of the house, filled with my own fears about winning favor in his eyes.

CHAPTER 12

Dusk has fallen. The bed is freshly made, pillows plumped, floors and windows scrubbed, and the lamps lit by the time I hear a carriage at the door. There's a commotion in the front hall. A deep voice booms a long string of instructions and insults to Reeve. I like Mr. Treadwell already.

The lady of the house is all high-pitched carrying-on. I smooth my maid's dress and check it for smudges and tears. I run my fingers through my hair to work out the worst of the knots. The lady of the house forbade me to cut it, so now it hangs down to my shoulders in the most revolting ringlets imaginable.

I take the back stairs with unladylike speed

thinking to give Cook a hand in the kitchen—or, if I'm honest, to sneak one of the biscuits I smelled her baking. But when I hit the second floor, curiosity gets the better of me and I tiptoe toward the parlor and all the commotion. I stand in the shadows just outside the parlor door.

The man of the house has magnificent black whiskers, a pearl-handled cane, and a travel-stained suit. He sits in the finest armchair with one freshly shined shoe up on the embroidered ottoman. I stifle a gasp. It's the fellow I spoke with on the street just this morning. I pray he won't recognize me in these clothes. He has a sparkly glass full of liquor and hands the lady of the house another. She waves it away. Temperance comes down the front stair while Kathleen emerges from the servant's stairway. Temperance hesitates at the door but Kathleen gives her a little nudge and she glides in.

"Ah, Temperance, you're a picture!" Mr. Treadwell says.

"Papa," she says with a curtsey. She gives her father a kiss on the cheek. "I didn't think you would be gone so long." She hesitates as is if she might say more but then goes to stand by the window.

Silence falls on the room as Mr. Treadwell sips

his drink and Mrs. Treadwell paces the floor and Temperance looks out at the street.

"Don't keep us in suspense, my love," the lady of the house says. "What news of our Valor?"

Just then, Reeve comes up with a tray of cold cuts and pickles. The lady of the house waves him in. Mr. Treadwell looks up wearily and shoos him away.

Reeve winces visibly but puts a brave face on it and walks into the room. He sets down the tray. "Cook will have dinner in an hour." He retreats with un-butler-like haste.

"Come eat something, dear. You must be famished."

"Famished," Mr. Treadwell says. "You don't know what hunger looks like." He drains his glass and pours another. "Take that away."

Mrs. Treadwell looks at the tray, perplexed. Kathleen takes a deep breath and glides into the room with her head down. She goes to the tray and scoops it up.

"I'll set it on the hall table just outside, ma'am," she says smoothly. "Under a napkin. In case himself changes his mind."

Mr. Treadwell takes another sip of whiskey and watches Kathleen walk away.

"Who is that?" he says.

"Nobody," the lady of the house answers quickly. "What news of Valor? Did you see him?"

The man of the house drains his liquor and pours another. "I've had no news at all of Valor, which is of course the best possible news."

"Best possible?" Mrs. Treadwell snaps. "You swore to me you'd find him. It's been months. Months since his last letter. He fought so bravely at Antietam, his letters so full of life and courage. He was everything we expected of him and then in December—"

"Right before Fredericksburg—" Temperance adds.

"Nothing!" the lady of the house wails. "Complete silence. I can't bear it! All the other mothers get letters from their sons. Fine letters, worthy of being read out at a tea or charitable committee meeting. Mrs. Kenton has had five letters from her son since Antietam. Four from Mrs. Dickenson's son, although her letters are longer and more elegantly descriptive. Oh, where can he be? How can he torture me so?"

This tirade gives Mr. Treadwell opportunity to finish his drink and start in on Mrs. Treadwell's glass.

Temperance turns back from the window. She goes to her father and pulls up a stool beside him. I glance at Kathleen. We shouldn't be listening. But it's so hard to walk away. There isn't a family in all of Ireland that hasn't had a son go missing one way or the other.

"Please tell us, Papa," Temperance says. "He wasn't on the death lists in the newspapers, but they get it wrong sometimes, don't they? Surely his friends know what's become of him. What do Paul Sanders and Billy Liles say?"

"And where have you been all these weeks, Elbridge?" Mrs. Treadwell barges in. "Why didn't *you* write me? I've been worn out with worry."

The man of the house puts his other foot up on the ottoman, his shoe shined to perfection below a travel-stained trouser leg. He leans back in the wing chair with a contented sigh. Mrs. Treadwell winces at the sight of the dirty clothes. I can't take my eyes off the brown crust of mud around his cuffs and the darker band of brown stain above it. I thought I'd never see the like of it again.

"A man does miss his own chairs when he travels." Mr. Treadwell raises the glass. "And the company of women."

He has a weary smile like the old soldiers in the pubs of Cork and Kerry. "When you are in enemy territory, my dear Mrs. Treadwell, a man does well not to communicate by something so easily stolen as a letter." He thumps his glass down on the side table and pours a generous refill.

"I have come from Chancellorsville."

I stifle a gasp. Yesterday I read in a thrown-out newspaper about a raging battle in Virginia. Thousands of men. Blazes of cannon fire. Bold charges. And heavy losses on all sides. I couldn't make out which side to root for and which to pity.

"There's none in Valor's unit who will speak of him. Hasn't been seen since Fredericksburg. No hospital has a record of him. He's not on a prisoner of war list."

The lady of the house staggers back a step and collapses onto a couch.

"He last drew pay after Fredericksburg. That is the long and short of it."

"Do you mean to say—our Valor? Could he be . . ."

"Gone."

"No."

"Deserted."

"Never! We did not raise him to disgrace his family."

I trade a glance with Kathleen. The English army had deserters too. There was money to be had in catching them if you could stomach the trade of bounty hunting.

"You don't know what that battlefield is like," the man of the house says, gazing blankly across the room. "I raised him to think on his feet and choose the path no one else has the courage to take." Mr. Treadwell turns to his wife. "Look around you, woman. Do you think I earned all this honorably? Do you think any man does when he deals in the machines of war? It's my cleverness you love, my instinct for opportunity. I gambled it all in one throw and I won. And here you are in your finery, with a house and servants as good as any on the block. Did you think our son would be different? If I know Valor, he's half way to the goldfields of Montana and traveling under a more suitable name."

The lady of the house opens and shuts her mouth like a landed trout. Temperance clasps her father's hand.

"Surely Paul and Billy would know if he meant

to run off and seek his fortune. Did you find them? What did they tell you?"

The man of the house closes his hand over hers.

"Paul is past all talking. And Billy, well, he denied he ever knew Valor. He's not the soft-spoken schoolboy you remember, Temperance. Desertion is a hanging crime."

Temperance shudders and looks away, but her father presses on.

"Billy can't claim to know Valor's plans. I wouldn't ask him to. Our Valor is gone and we will never know him by that name again. But don't despair. Maybe someday, a new man will come to us. One not polluted by this pestilent war. One I will take pride in, no matter what name he has chosen for himself."

Temperance blinks back tears.

"But you think he's alive?"

"I do."

"And Billy Liles? Is he alive too?"

"I saw him four days ago. A lot can happen in four days. Don't set your heart on a soldier, Temperance. War changes a man."

Temperance wrestles a handkerchief out of her sleeve and runs from the room. Kathleen starts to follow her, but the lady of the house motions us both into the room.

"Bridget, get us some tea please. And Mary, see that there is hot water for a bath."

She turns back to her husband. "Elbridge, don't frighten Temperance with your wild conjectures. She's at a delicate age."

"Frighten her?" he thumps his empty glass back on the table and pours another. "You are not frightened enough. I have walked three days across a battlefield. Seen the fruits of my business venture. These new rifles I've been selling the army, Zola, men fall in rows as they fight like stalks of wheat before the scythe. Do you know what this is?" He gestures toward his trouser legs. "Do you know, Zola?"

My heart is in my throat. Kathleen sees what I am seeing. She takes my hand to tug me back into the shadows of the hall, but I can't not remember. I can't not say it.

"Blood," I say. I'm shaking in my shoes when he turns my way. For what reason I cannot say, but I don't want him to feel alone. "When blood is in the puddles you walk through, it soaks in. The water dries but the blood stays."

A moment of such silence follows. It lasts for five full ticks of the hall clock. The Treadwells stare at me bewildered. I have said too much and not nearly enough.

When Ma went to get Packy's body from the wall behind the police station, she walked three miles on a rainy night to bring him home. Her skirt looked like Mr. Treadwell's trousers; a rime of mud at the bottom and a brown stain of blood above it. And her eyes wore the same soul-weary look as his do now.

The man of the house stands up and points a finger at me. There's no place to hide. What was I thinking to blurt out such a thing?

"Who the hell is this?" Mr. Treadwell says coldly.

"Now Elbridge—"

"And this?" He points at Kathleen. "What have you done, woman? Where is Martha? And Lucy?"

"Do sit down. Please. Eat something."

"Don't you try to feed me. Where are Martha and Lucy?"

"They—well—they weren't suitable."

"Not suitable? Lucy has been with us since Valor was a baby and Martha twice as long. *Where have they gone?*"

"Bridget and Mary are fine help. A credit to the household. Of course I was fond of Martha and Lucy, but look around, Elbridge. No one has black house servants. No one. Even folk with a thousand less a year than you don't keep them. If you were home more than a week at a time and attending all the society functions that I do, you would see for yourself. It's not that I have anything at all against those people. You know me, Elbridge. I am patriotic to the core. But it simply wouldn't be decent to keep them."

"Not decent? Not decent!"

Kathleen and I slowly back out of the room.

"We are fighting a war to free those people. Our son, our neighbors, our friends are dying for them."

"It's a war for . . . national unity," Mrs. Treadwell stammers. "To save the union."

Mr. Treadwell waves away her objection and pours himself yet another whisky. "Say what you will, Lincoln has freed the slaves. And when we win—never mind what the papers say, the North *will* prevail—where do you think *those folk* are going to live?"

"Surely Mr. Lincoln doesn't intend for them to move North." Mrs. Treadwell picks up a hand fan from the mantle and starts flapping herself to beat the band. "There will be laws to prevent it. Surely he intends for them to go west, where hardworking folk are needed."

The man of the house turns to his wife. He speaks softly but with the menace of a viper.

"Martha and Lucy have served us faithfully. I trust them. And I want them back. How dare you turn them out in the world without a friend to take them in? Who are you, to do such a thing? Have you forgotten where you come from? You weren't born to this." He waves an arm in the direction of the finery in the room. "And I'll tell you this. I liked you better back when you were scratching out a living, just like me. I miss that woman. She had a heart to her."

He turns abruptly, puts a steadying hand on the back of the chair. "And you!" he bellows to Kathleen and me. "Get out of my house. I want you gone before morning!"

He takes a few lurching steps toward us. We turn and run all the way up the back stair.

CHAPTER 13

"Daniel!" Kathleen sputters at me when we're behind the closed door of our attic room. "What were you thinking? Blood! Of all things to say!"

She yanks up the floorboard and starts frantically counting our wages. My knees give way and I lurch toward the cot, head spinning.

"Did you see the look on his face?" I whisper. "Heart-scalded, that's what he is. Weeks on the road, searching battlefields for the boy who's never coming home. He's like us. How can he be so rich and still be like us?"

"He's not like us," Kathleen snaps. She re-knots the money in her handkerchief and puts it in her pocket. "Would we put someone out on the street in the middle of the night?"

"What about Martha and Lucy? We're only here because she fired them. Just for being black. That's not fair."

"Who cares about them?" Kathleen takes me by both shoulders and gives me a shake. "They're from here. Somebody will take them in." She gives me another tooth-rattler. "You are my only responsibility. I won't lose you."

She gives me a hug to kill a more faint-hearted brother than me. I decide to tell her about my street dancing money before she squeezes all breath from my body. It's not a fortune, it won't keep us under a roof for long, but it's not the nothing we had when we came.

"Let me go!" I squirm out of her grasp. "Sit down, Kathleen," I begin. "I have something to say to you." I've not gotten another word out when Temperance bursts in the door.

"Bridget!" she cries. She's got a more woebegone expression than usual, and she's carrying a bundle of clothes under her arm. "Oh, Bridget, I'm so sorry. It's not your fault. Oh, but we did like Martha and Lucy. Loved them, really. They'd been with us for ever so long. And I was so cross with you because you weren't my Martha. But I couldn't just turn you out with nothing but the rags you came in. It wouldn't be right."

"I don't intend to leave in rags." Kathleen lifts her head. "I intend to leave in the clothes I'm wearing. The clothes your mother bought with my wages."

"That's not how things are done," Temperance says firmly, as though she is instructing a dolt. "A maid always leaves the dress behind for the next girl. You can have this one."

She thrusts a bundle of brown cloth into Kathleen hands.

"Ah," Kathleen says. "The brown serge you are so fond of wearing."

Last time Kathleen suggested Temperance wear this dress, she threw it across the room.

"I couldn't have you go away in tatters," Temperance goes on. "How do you expect to get a new position without a reference? Appearances are everything. The dress is yours! I shouldn't do it, but I will."

Kathleen sighs. She and Temperance are the same height but Temperance is considerably rounder. A fortnight of regular eating coupled with dawn-to-dusk labor has only knocked off Kathleen's sharp edges. She's still thin as a rail and scabby on the shins, like me. There's a week of needlework in re-making the dress to fit.

"Thank you," she says. Rich folk take a world of patience.

"And this is for you," Temperance says with a sly smile. She whips out a shirt and fine trousers just my size. "They were Valor's."

I make the most girlish gasp I can muster on the fly. I flap my hand at her instead of punching. "You must be teasing," I squeak, a full octave above middle C.

"What's this then?" Kathleen says, her expression a closed book.

"I saw him!" Temperance says triumphantly. "Sneaking out of the washing shed in trousers and a cap. What mischief are you up to, Mary—or whatever your name is?"

"You're mistaken," Kathleen says. "Must be some suitor of the Bridget across the way, come for a kiss in the morning. She's a beauty."

Did you ever hear such a smooth liar? I am brimming with admiration.

"I saw him, no mistake!" Temperance turns to me. "Don't you want proper boy clothes after all these weeks?" She waggles the trousers in front of me like you'd tease a dog with a bone. I hate her for having a thing to hold over my head and I want them, too. Thick, warm trousers, clean and pressed. I could dance across a Bowery stage in pants like that.

"Look at this face," Kathleen says, cupping my chin and squeezing my cheeks a bit to bring out the dimples. "Rosy cheeks and golden curls. God doesn't make boys like this."

Of all the things Kathleen has ever said to me, this one has teeth.

"Don't take them if you don't want," Temperance says, laying the shirt and pants on the bed. "But here's what you must give me in exchange."

Kathleen and I trade a wary glance. With charity there's always a price.

"You mustn't tell anyone about Father's drinking." She leans in as if someone could overhear us here at the top of the house. "No one can know. It would be such a disgrace. It's going to be hard enough to get a husband for me." She turns her face away. "Promise you won't tell."

Kathleen buckles our case shut. She stands, shoulders back and chin high. "Do you imagine that once we have left this house we will ever think of you again? Do my prospects seem so meager? You may think the lower classes look up to you, but trust me, Temperance, I will spend my whole life striving to be nothing like you."

I could stand up and cheer. I nearly do. Temperance gasps as though struck. She starts a retort but it dies in her throat.

"If you are quite finished, we must be on our way."

Temperance tries her best to pull herself together and leave the room with dignity, but I see tears brimming. She heads down the stairs like a whipped dog. If words were blows I'd put Kathleen up for prize fighting. I'm itching to ding a bell and raise her hand. But when I look at her, there's no victory.

"Bullocks," she says under her breath. It's the only curse she knows. She runs down the stairs after Temperance. While her back is turned, I snatch my dancing money out of its hiding place and tuck it safe under my skirt. I take Granny's bundle out from under the bed and follow her down the stairs.

"Wait!" Kathleen calls after her.

"I won't."

"Temperance, if your brother is truly gone— even if he's alive under another name—you are the heiress of this house."

"What?" Temperance stops, but she doesn't turn around.

"The only daughter of a wealthy man will not lack for suitors. You may have more of them than you'd care for."

"My mother—"

"Will see you in a new light. I won't lie to you— you're as plain as I am. But your new position gives you a power you did not have before."

"Power?"

"You can be the son he's lost. You don't have to be decorative now. Learn your father's trade. You are all he has."

There is a stretch of silence and then one set of footsteps continues downward. Feeling less triumphant than before, I meet Kathleen on the stairs with our case and bundle. We make our way to the back door without a word.

Cook is at the kitchen table with a glass of the wet and a foot up on a stool.

"Meddling rogue," she grumbles. "Trouble every time the man sets foot in the house. He'll be gone soon enough." She raises her glass. "But not soon enough for you." She gestures to a faded dishcloth on the table. It has a hearty oaten loaf and a whole wedge of her third-best cheese, and beside them a pair of chipped cups and a single wooden spoon.

"There's a relief kitchen down on Sixteenth Street." She ties the dishcloth together to make a bundle. "They have a decent soup, but it's better you bring your own cup."

I'm dumbfounded. She's one string of criticism when I'm standing over the dish tub. I thought she didn't like us at all. Before I can get a *thank you* out, I hear footsteps on the stair. Cook is out of her seat like a shot and closing the door to her room behind her.

The lady of the house sweeps into the kitchen. She has a wild look in her eye. "Stop right there!"

I freeze, but Kathleen slides in front of both me and Cook's bundle, giving me time to slip it off the table and out of sight.

"I simply can't have any interruption to my schedule," Mrs. Treadwell says. "A grand soirée does not plan itself." She clasps her hands together. "And I won't let my golden songbird fly away." She reaches toward me, all warm smile and pointy fingernails.

"But . . ." Kathleen puts a protective hand on my shoulder and it occurs to me that the lady of the house might keep me and send Kathleen away. I put my arm around my sister. My eye twitches over to the knife block.

"Mr. Treadwell will rise in the morning and go to seek our dear Martha and Lucy. Obviously we'll keep you two until he succeeds."

The lady of the house paces while Kathleen and I exchange worried looks.

"Of course he won't find them in that cesspool that lies below Fifteenth Street. He'll fume about it for a few days and then he'll make his deals and his visits to the bank. Before you know it, he'll be gone. Chasing the next golden opportunity."

Kathleen and I wait in silence, looking over her shoulder in case the master of the house turns up in an equally erratic frame of mind.

"So!" She clasps her hands together in satisfaction. "Disaster averted. You may return to your positions."

I loathe this woman more than ever. But if I'm honest, I was dreading going deep into the park where folk like us live in shacks made of garbage. The thought of standing on the sidewalk waiting in line for free soup and having to swear against my faith to get it fills me with shame.

"The man of the house has asked us to leave," Kathleen says. "So surely we must go."

What can she be thinking? I give her a warning pinch.

"Don't be ridiculous," Mrs. Treadwell says. "It's the middle of the night and you have nothing. You'll be beggars in the street just like you were in Ireland. Do you want your sister to starve?"

"I will never let her starve," Kathleen says. "Never. And we won't be on the street for long. My quick needlework and her golden voice will find employment that pays better than this."

"Oh, is that what this is about? More money? You chiseler! I pay you a fair wage."

"You pay me seventy-five cents a week and the going wage is a dollar. I can read the newspaper, ma'am."

"You grasping wretch. I took you from the gutter! I won't give you a trime more than you're getting now."

"Oh no? I have it on good authority from the Bridget three doors down that Mrs. Liles is looking for help. You know how much that woman loves music."

The lady of the house goes pale.

"And gossip," I add, remembering Temperance's attempt at a bribe.

Mrs. Treadwell puts a steadying hand on a chair. "Anyone would think you're gypsies the way you bargain," she says. "Ninety cents a week. Now up the stairs you go, and quietly if you know what's good for you."

"I do know what's good for me, good for us both." Kathleen takes a big breath and holds my hand in hers. "And I will not accept being deprived of the practice of my faith." For just a moment Kathleen's voice wavers with emotion. "I will bring my sister up in the faith of my family. We will go to the Catholic church of my choosing and remain there until noon every Sunday and holy days, too, so that we may receive education, good fellowship, and the sacraments that my family has bled and died for."

I am not such a saint that I miss the study of the Bible, but until this moment I did not remember how much I miss being in church—in beauty and peace and music. Prayers I know by heart and people. People who care for me, not for my labor, but for myself.

I close my eyes and sing my mother's favorite hymn. I let the *Ave Marias* ring out as pure and clear as I know how.

"All right! Fine. Agreed," the lady of the house says. She shoos us in the direction of the back stair.

We scamper up like a pair of thieving mice and Kathleen is gasping, almost laughing with relief by the time we get to the top.

"Oh Danny boy!" she says. "You're brilliant! She nearly wept. It's like a magic power you have in that voice."

She laughs, scoops me up in her arms, and swings me around like she hasn't since . . . I can't even remember how long.

"That's not all," I say with glee. "Shall we dine?" I open up Cook's dishtowel and there is fresh cheese and a sweet oaten loaf, not the flavorless pale one she makes for the lady of the house—real bread, hearty like they make it in Ireland. And it's still warm.

CHAPTER 14

SUNDAY, MAY 10, 1863

The next morning, Kathleen returns Temperance's gift of clothes without a word. Temperance doesn't tell her parents I'm a boy. Kathleen doesn't tell the neighbors that Mr. Treadwell is a drunk. There's a chilly sort of respect between them as they soldier on through her dress fittings and hair styling.

Two days later, Kathleen and I walk side by side in our clothes from home, all washed and mended for Sunday. I don't mind wearing Granny's dress so much this time. It feels like home. I'm so busy every minute of the day, between the eternal round of scrubbing and keeping out of sight of the man of the house, that I go for hours, a whole day sometimes, without thinking of my family. And then I am more homesick for forgetting them.

New York is fine in May, trees in the park leafy, and the last sooty lumps of snow melted away. Flowers fight their way up through the mud and gravel. Kathleen revels in it. I throw a skip-two-three into my walk just to see if I can get her to dance with me. We used to dance the two-hand reel when we were little, but Kathleen hates to have eyes on her.

We start through the park at sunrise and take our leisurely time walking the two and a half miles to St. Francis Xavier. I still haven't told Kathleen about the dancing money so I pretend that everything we're seeing is new to me. She is bursting with curiosity, and I realize with shame that she has never been away from the Treadwell house, not once in the six weeks we've lived there. Her whole life has shrunk to one city block.

Lucky for me, the shops are all closed on Sunday, so there's nobody who might recognize me at the greengrocer's or the butcher's.

I spy the bootblack who wouldn't take my coin of apology, but his head is bent over shoes and he doesn't see Kathleen and me pass by.

The farther south we go, the more people look like us. There are fewer top hats and fur collars. Men in soft plaid caps and women with their shawls wrapped around them walk arm in arm, trailing strings of blue-eyed children. The only workers on the street are the newsboys. They come pouring uptown from the print shops.

"Chancellorsville! Death lists today!" they shout.

People open their windows. They stream out their doors with pennies in hand. When the newsboys run out, people share the pages around. Some gasp sighs of relief and some turn away weeping. The black street sweepers and tub men walk on by, paying the commotion no mind. Kathleen puts an arm around my shoulder.

"You are never joining the army, Danny. I won't have it."

I slip my arm around her waist and we keep walking down Fifth to Madison Square. With every step I think of Eliza's boy, Michael, and the grocer's boy, Jackie. By the time we hit Twentieth Street, weeping and moaning can be heard from every tenement window. A family of five stands on a corner poring over the page. The father gives a shout of triumph, the little sisters hug each other and jump for joy, the mother wipes her streaming eyes.

As we draw near the church on Sixteenth Street I hear more and more Irish accents. There's the soft refined talk from South Dubliners, and the singsong voices of Connacht men. Two lads are speaking so thick and deadly fast I can barely tell if they're speaking English or no. Those'll be Kerry men. But no matter the accent, the draft is all their talk. Will it come next week? Next month? Will they take older men with families? Boys of sixteen or seventeen years? The papers don't agree and speculation spreads like a fire.

The death list is posted on the door of St. Francis Xavier. It's seven pages long—more than 10,000 names. I should look for Eliza's son, but I couldn't bear to bring her the news.

Kathleen draws her shawl up over her head like women do to cover their hair in church. She frets over mine until it's to her liking and then we go up the long side aisle with the colored light from the windows slanting across the floor. We find a spot and Kathleen goes to her knees at once, but I'm so weighed down by that long list of dead men. It sits on my shoulders and I can't think what to pray. All around me folk are weeping, young and old alike, calling the names of their dead, or staring into the distance in shock with no words at all. A hundred or more people file in—some Germans and Italians in with us Irish.

The familiar words of the Mass wash over me. It's been almost six months since we last went to a Mass at St. Michael on the dockside of Cove. Sometimes you don't miss a thing until you find it again.

After Mass, Kathleen puts a penny in the poor box and we go to the parish hall. The nuns serve a fine meal of colcannon and soda bread. The folks sitting by us are abuzz with talk of the war. A fellow by the name of Doyle is reminding the newcomers that it was only a few years ago when the Know Nothing mobs marched through cities, burning Catholic churches and orphanages and Irish neighborhoods.

"They'll be back," Doyle says. "If we don't serve our country as volunteers, if we don't take the hardest duty and fight better than that Protestant rabble, they'll use it as a stick to beat us with for the rest of our lives!"

"And how long will any of us live if we keep

sending our men to the slaughter?" A red-haired woman says. She's been holding her own against Doyle even with the babe in arms.

"You're too old to serve, Doyle. Don't you speak for us men of fighting age," says a lad not much older than Kathleen.

"Look at her there," the woman says, nodding toward a mother with three children who are standing by a closet at the back of the hall. One of the nuns is parceling out oats and sugar to her. Another is holding up a dress to the middle child, who is nearly in rags. "Maureen was barely managing on a soldier's pay. Now she's got nothing, and all those hungry little ones. Another at home, sick with a fever and no money for the doctor. You're a fine one to talk about gaining respect. No wife or child of your own. I'll take my child's life, thank you. The respect of Protestants—that's a fool's errand."

I look from one angry face to the next. I thought America was going to be different. I thought we would never be afraid, what with all the freedoms. Kathleen puts a warning hand on my arm, so I don't bust out and say something boyish.

"At least we have the vote here," the young man says. "We never did in Ireland."

"At least we have a school of our own," the woman adds.

Kathleen squeezes my arm at the mention of a school.

"That's what I want for my son," the woman says taking hold of her baby's tiny hand. "A proper school where he can learn the same as everyone else, without having to say Protestant prayers."

The talk goes on and on. Boys drift away to play marbles in the corner. I'm good at that game. Won a real glass marble off a town boy once with a marble I made out of clay. The girls do hopscotch on the brown and gray floor stones. I never played the girl's games at home. I could do it, though. Better than them, I bet. I slide into line for a turn.

"Fifteen is too old for such games," Kathleen says in my ear.

She takes me by the elbow and steers me down the hallway to look at the pictures of the saints on the wall. As if that's a better game! We find a classroom that's not locked.

"Will you look at it, Daniel?" Kathleen says. "Everything you need. Everything you could possibly want!" She waves an arm at the chalkboard, a stack of slates and pencils, a map of the States. She walks over to the bookshelf. "Books! A dozen of them. History. Science. Think of it!"

At home our hedge master never had more than one book, and never a large one to attract attention. He'd take any book he could easily hide, and we'd read out of it in turns. We'd write the sums and letters with a stick in the mud. And we'd scatter at a word, if the police were abroad in the lane. I got on well enough with the lessons, but Kathleen was the star pupil. He filled her head with grand visions of how a school could be in a free country.

"What's this, then?" I say, pointing to a thick book on the teacher's desk.

"*A Compendious Dictionary of the English Language*," she reads. "Isn't it grand!" She flips past the page with the bewhiskered fellow in the black suit and the curling letters of the title. "Aardvark," she announces with great authority. "Noun. A large burrowing nocturnal mammal of sub-Saharan Africa." She runs her finger down the page. "Accipiters. Noun. An order of fowls with hooked beaks. Advocate. Verb. To defend, plead in favor of."

The door opens abruptly, and a nun wreathed in layers of black slides into the classroom and closes the door. "A scholar," she says.

Kathleen snaps the book shut. She steps away from the table, eyes darting around the room but the nun—a tall, solid-looking one—stands in front of the only door.

"I'm sorry . . . I didn't . . . I shouldn't . . ." Kathleen steps away from the dictionary and backs herself into a corner. I step in front of Kathleen, scanning the windows in the hope of escape.

"She didn't do any harm, Sister. None at all."

"Indeed," the nun says, neither frowning nor smiling. "You will come with me please."

She turns and walks away, the rope that ties at her waist swinging back and forth like a scolding finger. We follow her in fear of our salvation. We cross a brick courtyard with a statue of the Blessed Mother, a row of vegetables, one lone tree and a brick convent on the far side. The sister leads us all the way to the end of the third-floor corridor. We walk into a parlor as fine as any room in the Treadwells' house. She dips a hand in the holy water by the door and crosses herself, so we do the same.

"Do sit, children."

She goes behind a desk, the sound of her footsteps lost in a fine warm carpet. We perch on her chairs. A band of sunlight from a tall window lights us up and leaves her in shadow.

"I am Mother Hildegard. May I make your acquaintance?"

"Kathleen O'Carolan, Mother."

I can't use my real name, but I'm pretty sure lying to a nun is a bigger sin than your ordinary everyday kind of lying. I miss a beat before stammering out, "Mary."

She continues to look at us, neither smiling nor frowning. I feel a sudden desire to confess the truth, all out of step with my usual impulses.

"We've done you no harm," I say to hold off the urge. "She's after liking books. Nothing more."

"Nothing more?"

"I'm sorry," Kathleen stammers, beet red in the face. I've never seen her so flustered. "I won't do it again."

"Won't you?" Mother Hildegard says in a deceptively mild voice.

Oh, she's a clever one.

"I suspect the classroom draws you. Does it not? Do you think often upon the allure of books and learning?"

I scoot over and give Kathleen a warning pinch.

"I don't—I do." Kathleen squirms in her chair. "I can resist it. I will."

Jesus and his flaming heart are staring us down from a picture frame over Mother Hildegard's shoulder. The holy water is still moist on my fingertips and forehead. She could draw truth out of us like a barber draws blood. I can feel it.

"I am certain you could resist almost anything," Mother Hildegard says. "You have the look of a great resister."

She doesn't know the half of it.

"The question before you, Kathleen, is this. Is the classroom a temptation or an invitation?" She holds Kathleen in her gaze for long ticks of the tall clock behind us. At last Kathleen drops her eyes.

"There is time for the considering of this question," Mother Hildegard says. "You are not such a concern to me as your brother there."

Kathleen gasps. I look down at my dress, my button-up girl shoes. My hands are even folded in my lap the way a girl does it. All my breath whooshes out. What hope was there for me ever? I turn to Kathleen, angry now.

"I did everything you told me! You said nobody would ever guess." I hop out of my chair and pace long strides in front of Mother Hildegard's desk. "I did everything right!" I shout. "I'm not even wearing pants under!"

I lift up the edge of my skirt and scandalize Mother Hildegard with a bare ankle. She takes a handkerchief out of her sleeve and holds it over her mouth. But she's not coughing. She's smiling behind there. I could take that teacup on her desk and smash it, I'm so mad.

"I have this!" I hold out my curls like two tails of pig. "And this!" I plaster on my biggest smile and point to the dimples.

Mother Hildegard is not even hiding her smile now.

I worked so hard. It's not fair that she can tell I'm a boy. "How did you know?" I fold my arms across my chest and stare her down, her and the Sacred Heart on the wall, too.

"The body is easily disguised; the heart, less so. Back in the classroom, when you perceived a danger to your sister, what did you do?" She pauses while I remember the awful truth. "Without thought or hesitation you placed your body, small as it is, between her and harm's way."

I could spit.

"Oh *liebchen*," she says softly. "You are ringed about by the men of your family, however far away they may be. And they are teaching you to be a man in this world, in spite of your current disguise."

I manage to rein in the spit, but can't help a prideful huff.

"Grace is hard to resist, Little Mule." She says tucking the handkerchief back in her sleeve. "Says one who has fought against it long and vigorously, and to no avail."

"Don't take him from me, Mother," Kathleen says. She hops up from her chair and kneels right there on the floor. "Give me what penance you will. I'm the one who made him to dress this way. He's all the family I've got. I swore on the names of Jesus and Mary that I'd protect him."

She looks up, pleading.

"Rise up now, young lady," Mother Hildegard says. "I have the utmost respect for vows taken. But you must understand that a vow undertaken in the depth of sorrow at a moment when you are bereft of power does not have the same moral force as a vow taken joyfully after long and careful thought."

"I won't let him go! I can't!"

"Long indeed would be the crowbar I would need to pry him from you." Mother Hildegard comes around from behind her desk, takes Kathleen by the shoulders, and sits her down. "Come now." She settles the long folds of her habit into the opposite chair. "I am a great lover of stories, and you two are brimming over with a lively tale. Tell me."

Just like that Kathleen spills the whole thing, from our first landing two months ago. I sound braver in the telling than I ever felt in the living of it.

"Have you anything to add?" she says to me when Kathleen is finished.

"I hate dresses. I hate lying. But I won't go back to sleeping in ditches and rooting through garbage. I won't go to the poorhouse."

Mother holds up a hand in benediction. "Your poverty mitigates the sin of the lie."

I glance over at Kathleen. She's a great one for long words. She gives me a shrug.

"Mitigate," Mother Hildegard says, gently. "Verb. To cause to become less harsh, to make less severe or painful. Next time you are in my classroom, you should look up clemency. Noun. A disposition to be merciful." She leans toward Kathleen and takes her hand. "I will not turn your 'sister' over to the orphan asylum. Your employers are far from perfect, and yet they are less brutal than some. Yes?"

We both nod, worn out in our relief.

"But we must look for a better position for you, one where you can both live without the burden of the lie you have placed upon your brother. This disguise cannot hold forever. And there is cruelty in forcing him to pretend to be what he is not. We must look together for a better way."

"I will," Kathleen says. "I promise."

And when we walk out in the sunlight, the comfort of sharing our truth with one sympathetic ear lifts us up. I skip the full length of a block and Kathleen skips right beside me.

CHAPTER 15

MONDAY, JUNE 29, 1863

Next morning while I'm shopping for Eliza, I think over what Mother Hildegard said. It does feel like a trap to be a girl at the Treadwells' house. It's not just the wearing of the dress. There's a way to walk and sit and answer back your betters when you're a girl. Everything I do as a girl feels small—short steps when I walk, little mouthfuls of food, a sip instead of a gulp, giggling where a full-out laugh should go. It's so much work to hold myself in. I don't know how any girl does it.

And I'm in a terror to get it wrong and be found out. Eliza has proven worthy of my trust and Kathleen counts Jane as a friend, but none of the rest can resist gossip. And that Alice across the way has vinegar for blood and a viper's tongue. She has no pity in her at all. None for the beggar children who come round the alley looking for scraps. None even for the fugitive slaves that the slave catchers drag away in chains. How is that different from the crimes Cromwell did to us in his day? There's no understanding her. I think she likes it when someone is brought low. If she knew I was a boy she'd rip me to shreds. I do my best to fit in, pretending to be shy and talking as little as possible.

I'd go mad if I didn't have my mornings at the market. Today I see that bootblack on the corner by the grocery. A man with gray hair, spectacles, and shabby shoes walks past him but then turns back. "Samuel, is that you?"

The bootblack looks up but doesn't smile. "Mr. Avrim, sir. Shine your shoes, sir?" He doesn't stand to greet this Avrim who knows his name.

Avrim looks at his feet. "There's little left of them to shine," he says. "If only I were a cobbler and not a tailor, you'd have a better shoe to work with."

I set down the cabbages I'm buying and slide over for a closer look. I've seen this fellow before. He's got the tailor shop a few blocks down.

"On the other hand," Avrim says. "I have a nickel left over from the dry goods."

"You put your foot there, sir," Samuel says.

Avrim puts his foot on the box and Samuel gets to work.

"What became of your carpentry?" Avrim says.

"Dismissed from service," Samuel says. It costs him in pride to say it, I can tell.

"A pity. And such good work as yours," Avrim says. "But you have the tools yet?"

"Yes, sir," Samuel says.

I don't know why this Avrim fellow has to ask. A working man would never let go his tools. He'd trade his own bed and coat for food before he'd give them up. Da's tool handles were black with the sweat of the three generations of O'Carolans who worked the trade before him. He tended them like you'd tend a garden. Each one clean and sharp, ready for whatever job came along.

This fellow is a craftsman. I can tell by the care he takes with each shoe. Same care he gave to those rich swells goes to this man who clearly doesn't live in a grand house or command servants. I'm certain this fellow has a fine set of tools. I'd stake a whole dime on it.

When Avrim's shoes are clean, he steps off the box. He presses a nickel in Samuel's hand. "Big Al is still building that theater down in the Bowery. He needs another carpenter."

Samuel stands up. He brushes the dirt from his hands. "And he's willing to lose the carpenter he has to hire me? You know an Irishman won't willingly work beside me. Why should I risk stirring up trouble?"

"Big Al is the persuasive type," Avrim says. "He could talk a tiger out of his stripes. And he goes to church every Sunday with all the Irish in the Bowery. He knows how to appeal to their better nature."

"I'll see evidence of this better nature before I believe it," Samuel says.

"The plasterers are Italian, the painters are German and it's true the brickwork is done by the Irish, but our lead carpenter is one of your own. You'd get on, I think, and he could use the help. Will you try?"

I lean in waiting for Samuel to answer. Hoping that he'll say yes. Imagining the world of trouble and loneliness I'd be in if every other maid and washerwoman scorned the very sight of me.

Samuel turns the shoe brush over and over in his calloused hands. Avrim puts a hand on his shoulder.

"This other carpenter, Isaac by name, he's the only black man working for Big Al. If it was your brother down there, would you want him to be alone?"

Samuel sighs but then he smiles. "You were saying about the tiger and his stripes?"

Avrim shrugs. "Not every man will fix a broken window when the shop belongs to a Jew. It's a blessing to me to help a righteous man."

"Thank you," Samuel says. He picks up his shine box and walks toward the park with a bit of spring in his step.

I watch him go, thinking of the nightmare I get these days. I'm standing before the ocean. A great wave rises up and I run from it. But the faster I run the bigger it grows. I can hear it roaring, feel it throwing a shadow over me, but it's too big to fight, and I wake up drenched in the sweat of it. Sometimes even when I'm awake I can hear that roar and feel that shadow behind me. I reckon I'm not the only one scrambling for my life.

★★★

Mr. Treadwell leaves the next morning. The lady of the house says he's been called away on business, but Kathleen saw him pack up a case of Valor's clothes, and every kind of medicine that money can buy. I'd bet half of my pennies that he's gone to Montana and he's never coming back.

You'd think Mrs. Treadwell would be upset on his leaving but it's only Miss Temperance who sheds a tear. The lady of the house is dead set on her soirée. She stokes the anxieties of the household until we are a near-bonfire of new dresses, elegant teacake recipes, and refined music.

Weeks roll past and New York gets hotter in every possible way. Muddy puddles harden, crack, and release a relentless brown dust upon the laundry line. The smell of trolley horse manure that I hardly noticed in March is inescapable in June.

Bitter war news rolls in from Vicksburg and Virginia. Camp fever and ague strikes every brigade from Pennsylvania to Tennessee. Arguments about the draft and whose name will be in the hopper break out in pubs and spill over onto the streets. The fire brigades are in the thick of it. There's no exemption for firemen. And if they go to the battlefield, who will fight the fires that break out in factories and tenements and tall ships? I can see them from my attic window. The fire bell rings and smoke rises somewhere in the city every single day.

The prices of food and coal soar up overnight. Mrs. Treadwell can't get Reeve a fancy new butler's coat because Brooks Brothers is sewing army uniforms and they've used every scrap of wool in town. The grocer and the butcher run short every other day, leaving respectable women hissing at each other like alley cats over a bunch of cabbages or a rasher of bacon. Even the barber, the most buoyant spirit in the neighborhood, has given up on love songs entirely. For weeks now he's been singing about a fellow, name of Don Giovanni, who gets dragged into hell by a demon on account of sins so egregious the barber will only sing about them in Italian.

The sun rises so early now that I have the devil's own time to slip out of the house in disguise before folks are afoot. But I take the risk over and again because Eliza's limp is steadily worse. She has a growing fear of being let go from service. Replaced with a younger Bridget. How would her Michael ever find her then? Kathleen and I find little ways to ease her burden, even as she secretly eases mine.

I'd give in to despair if couldn't go about in my right clothes some of the time.

Even when the city is a powder keg, I have come to love New York. Every time I walk to the market I pass new faces, see new goods in the shop windows, hear languages from countries I cannot guess. And songs! There's not a grand house that doesn't have a piano, and in summer, some folk are kind enough to keep the windows open when they play. The cigar factory is a music factory too; one roller sings to his fellows, another sings back. Musters of soldiers camped in the park sing out marching jodies as they drill. I drink it all in with eager ears. And every chance I get, I look for my old soldier on Sixtieth Street and dance to his harmonica tunes.

Over the weeks I notice some repeat listeners in my audience. Most of them Irish, with a keen eye for my footwork. But soldiers stop by too. Men on leave, or mustered out, and more and more as spring turns to summer, bandaged-up men with crutches.

One Monday morning I notice a man who has been there before. Now that I think on it, he's been there at least twice. Always wearing a topcoat and tall hat with a fine silk tie. He stands off to the side where he can hear me, but he never looks at me. He looks at my audience.

I take a break from dancing and the old soldier plays "Aura Lee"—a tune that everyone in town can chime in on. I give the fellow in the top hat a good look, wondering what I might sing to tempt him out of a coin. He's a music lover, I'm sure, but probably not one to win over with "Beautiful Dreamer" or "Arkansas Traveler."

I'm so busy thinking, I don't see the army officer until he's right in front of me. He's got the gold braid over his shoulder and three stripes up and three down on his sleeve. I'm not sure what all the ranks are, but the more stripes, the more money he's got for tips.

"You're a regular champion of the rhythms," he says to me.

"Thank you," I say, anticipating a decent-sized coin and prepared to chat a little to get it.

"Have you ever played a drum?"

"I have not."

"Would you like to learn?"

"My two feet are all the drum I need."

"Come join the Highlander's Brigade and you can have a drum for free. I'll teach you to play."

I hesitate. Patriotism is popular, even as the war has gotten so much harder. I don't want to put paying customers off.

"I couldn't possibly join the army. My ma would take it so."

"If you come with me now you'll get a signing bonus for your mother. Ten dollars," he says. "Ten!"

I pause for breath. All that money in one go! I don't want to be in the army, but I won't lie: I want ten dollars. The glimmer of so many coins dazzles me, but only for a moment. "I gave Ma my word."

"Don't be a fool, boy," the officer says, stepping closer. "The draft is coming." He lowers his voice. "Names will be drawn in a few short days and then the signing bonuses will be done. You have this one chance to put a fortune in your mother's hand."

I take a step back from him, all hope of a coin vanished.

"I need a drummer. You could be one of us. One of those chosen for greatness. A drummer with a steady cadence like yours, why, he calls the men to battle. Keeps them in step on the road. Tells them which way to turn when the smoke is so thick you can't see your way home. You could save lives."

His voice rings out over the group of listeners, not because he has spoken louder, but because the old soldier has stopped playing in the middle of the song. He gets up without speaking and hobbles over to stand between me and the officer. There's no need for words from my silent partner. He wears a look to melt iron.

"Come to vouch for the lad? Is he a good worker?" The officer tries a jovial approach, but they look at each other like circling dogs.

Another man steps out of the crowd and stands by the old soldier's side. He's speckled with wood shavings and wears a carpenter's apron. "I heard this boy tell you no," he says.

"It's no business of a man who's never served his country."

"Here's a man who's done his bit for the Union and heard the boy tell you no." A man from the back of the audience steps forward. He lifts his cap to the officer and turns his head to show the bubbly scar of a powder burn over the side of his face. "Even with this ear!" He points to the crumpled remains of a right ear.

Two more men step out of the crowd and silently stand in the row to defend me.

"Fools," the officer says. "Lincoln needs soldiers and he'll have them. All of you should sign up today and get your bonuses. When the draft comes you'll get nothing."

My row of defenders stand resolute and stare the man down.

The butcher's son, Ivan, sees the standoff and comes across the street from his shop, meat cleaver in hand and shoulders like an ox. "What's going on here?" he says.

A woman with a shopping basket points an accusing finger at the officer. "That vulture there is trying to recruit our little man with the golden voice."

"Don't take him from us," another woman says. "You've taken our men already. You'll leave us the boys."

"'Tis ashamed you should be," shouts a Galway man. "'Tis always the Irish you're after to pay the butcher's bill. In a war not our own."

People from the park and across the street come over and join the audience. I feel like I'm standing at the bottom of a cliff at the beginning of a landslide. The men, even the women around me, are a humming hive of anger.

"Take your own son if you want a drummer!"

"He's only a child!"

"Keep him out of it! Keep all our sons out of it!"

Ivan the butcher leans close to me and says, "This could go sideways, lad. Tempers are hot all over town. Run along to your ma now before the coppers come."

The crowd parts for me and then closes the recruiter in its hard fist of outrage. I hear a policeman's whistle and the urge to run takes hold of me. But John always said running is how the policemen caught our Packy. So I force myself to walk.

A second police whistle sounds and then a third. A block away from the crowd I breathe a bit easier. Three coppers come running up the street. I step into a doorway and they pass me by. I see that two of them have red hair and the third is calling orders to his mates in an accent straight out of Donegal. I didn't know a policeman could be Irish. I blow out a huge sigh of relief, and then the man with the top hat steps into the doorway, blocking my way out.

"You've had quite a morning," he says.

Ordinarily I'd chat up a patron and get a coin out of him for my trouble. But today I'm wary.

"What do you want?"

"Be easy now. I mean you no harm."

"I should go home."

"May I come with you and meet this mother to whom you are so devoted?"

This is a trick. It's some sort of trap. Maybe another recruiter, chosen for his dapper style and boyish face.

"My ma's working," I say. "Everybody's ma is working. What do you want with her?"

"Of course she is," the man says, not at all put off by my sass. "I have what you'd call a business proposition for your family."

I do not like the sound of that.

"I've never quite seen the like of you," he goes on. "Street-corner singers are ten a penny. But you are a puzzle to me. You have a trained voice, I'd wager a month's rent on it. And yet you don't stick to the dusty classics a society household prides its self on. Each time I've listened, you've had a new song to sing. Something folks lean into. Something they can hum along. That's showmanship, and it's rare in a performer twice your age."

I look for a way to edge past the man, but he's wide as well as tall.

"There are many good singers in this world. A few of them can even dance. But you, my little Irishman, have moved a crowd of strangers to stand in your defense. That is more rare than you can know. Audience loyalty can't be bought. It's carefully built—over years, sometimes. And here you've worked the magic all on your own without a soul to help you."

He pauses to let that thought sink in.

"Would you like a real audience? A proper stage to dance upon and a regular wage?"

"I'm no saloon girl to be dancing in a room full of drunken grabbers!"

The man smiles. He takes off his hat and holds it over his heart. "I never liked the dance hall trade. I have a new theater now, nearly finished. No bar at all. A proper place with a respectable stage where families can come, children and all, when their working day is done. Singing and dancing to lift the soul! Animal acts and jugglers to astound the senses!"

I squirm in my shoes. Them devils in there love the idea of theater work. But Kathleen would flay me alive for taking to the stage.

"I have to go home," I say.

"Indeed you do," the man says with a smile. "Please, allow me to present three tokens of my sincerity."

He holds up a coin, a whole silver dollar.

"This is for the dancing today. As fine a hornpipe as ever I've seen, and I've seen a few."

Next he reaches in his breast pocket and draws out a small piece of fine paper.

"When your mother and father are ready to meet me and hear the contract I will offer, show this card to any cab driver in the city and they will take all of you to this address. I will pay your fare, however far it may be."

I take the card from his hand. It says *Big Al's Variety Theater* in curly letters. A wreath of flowers surrounds his name. Below, it says *Canal Street and the Bowery.*

"And finally," Big Al says with a flourish, "this." He hands me the old soldier's tin cup, half full of pennies. "You left this behind in the ruckus."

He looks me in the eye, this Big Al. He has a wise look to him but not a sharp one. A pleading look, not a threatening one.

"It's not all my money," I say. "Half belongs to the old soldier."

"Count out your share then and I'll see the rest safely home to him." Big Al puts the can in my hand. "Do you trust me?"

God help me. I do. I count out my share of pennies and tuck them in a pocket. "I'll talk to my family and see what they say."

"That's all I ask."

Big Al steps aside. I run down the street, pennies jangling in my pocket and a silver dollar held fast in my hand.

**LOCAL INTELLIGENCE: THE DRAFT.
THE ENROLLMENT COMPLETED.**
Twenty-five Thousand Men to be Drawn in the City,
and Seven Thousand in Brooklyn.

—*New York Times*

CHAPTER 16

SATURDAY, JULY 11, 1863

I've spent a whole week working up the nerve to tell Kathleen about the audition. I love the idea of putting a whole dollar in her hand. But she's a sharp one with questions. She's heard plenty of dark tales from the other Bridgets about girls who went wrong working in those concert saloons. Maybe Big Al will offer a decent wage and we can find a place to live among our own. But what if he doesn't? The pay could be no better, and the food and rooms worse.

In the end I decide to tell her nothing until I've sniffed things out. I spend another week looking for a chance to get away from the house.

Mrs. Treadwell's grand soirée is only a few days away. She and Mrs. Vanderzanden have worked themselves into a froth of worry because everyone is upset over the dreadful news coming out of Pennsylvania and Virginia. Invitation returns cascade into the mailbox from folks who have left town for the summer. Reeve is sent out again and again with more invitations on even fancier paper. The music master has been coming three times a week and Temperance is in tears of anxiety by the end of every lesson.

Cook grumbles about the state of her kitchen with me in lessons every other day, but she opens the kitchen door when I practice my songs over the washtub. Every cook and lady's maid on the block does the same.

The Bridgets are a flurry of gossip in the alleys. The Irish Brigade fought valiantly at Gettysburg and Chancellorsville. Everyone agreed they did. Two-thirds of the brigade died in those battles—near a thousand men all told and more than twice as many maimed. Would they be called to lead the charge in battle again? Would they come home alive?

Eliza is the only one who will have no part of the gossip. "What good will any of it do?" she says over her tub of washing on a Friday morning. "It's gone from my hand he is, and God alone can carry my son back to me."

I don't know what to say to her. God has a lot of folk to carry these days and it's plain to see some of them are getting dropped.

It's scorching hot in the alley already and the gossip rages on.

"It's them rich swells that never pay the price of it," Alice from across the alley says. She mops the back of her neck with a wet cloth.

"And the black workers aren't pulling their weight either," says Ann from next door. "Not a single one of them in the hopper for the draft. Where's the fairness of that?"

"Why should we die for their freedom?" Alice says. "When did they ever defend us from the English who butchered us like sheep and stole our land? Let them find some other country and start new, same as us!"

Heads nod over the washtubs. It's true; nobody ever came to Ireland to help us in our troubles. It feels right that other folk should help their own.

"Sure, it's always the same. The Irish are treated like dogs, no matter where they go," Bridget chimes in.

"It's not our war," Alice says going pink with anger as much as sun. "If black men want their freedom, let them fight and die for it, same as us."

"Black workers are treated like dogs, too, if you hadn't noticed," Jane says in her firm but quiet way. "And they're not fighting because they're not *allowed* to fight. No one wants to see a gun in a black man's hand, so they only let them be cooks and nurses in the army."

"Is that true?" I say under my breath. I lean over Jane's fence to not call attention.

"I spoke with Martha about it before she was dismissed," Jane says. "Her man was keen to fight and went to Massachusetts to join a colored brigade there."

"She has a man?" I say, still whispering.

"'Course she has a man, and children, too. Star pupils at the Colored Orphan Asylum to hear tell of it. She was sad to take them from school, but glad enough to bring her family together under one roof at last."

Massachusetts. Poor Mr. Treadwell was looking in entirely the wrong direction. He'll never find Martha now. Looks like she doesn't even want to come back. I won't lie—it's a load off my conscience to think of Martha with her own family in Massachusetts instead of homeless in New York.

The rest of the Bridgets fan their ruddy faces with their aprons and swat at flies.

"I saw a blackbirder, not three weeks ago," says Jane. "Captured a black man in broad daylight and clapped him in chains. They'll sell that man South. They will. Why he's no more than a mule to such men. It's a cruel thing—bad as any transportation the English did to us."

"Whatever we do we have to keep the vote," Peg says sternly, as she pins diapers on the line. "It's our only power. Them fools down at the Tammany Hall won't be finding jobs for us if our men don't have a vote."

"There won't be an Irishman standing to cast a vote if the war keeps up," says Ann.

"It's a sin to turn our backs on black folk who suffer just as we have," Jane says. "Shame on us if we do. Martha was a good woman and kind to us all. Have you forgotten her so soon?"

"She brought me cups of broth whenever I was ill," Eliza says.

Bridget hangs her head for shame. Ann too. Jane takes a handful of green beans from her garden and hands it over to the hollow-eyed newsboy lurking in the alley—the one who sometimes sleeps behind our trash bins.

"Easy for you to say," Peg says to Jane, throwing the diaper water into the gutter. "You don't have a brother in uniform or a husband working on the docks. Don't forget it was black workers who broke the strike. Shame on them!"

"And were they allowed to join the union same as our men? Were they?" Jane turns on her heel and goes inside. I've never seen her lose her temper like that.

I don't know what to think. I don't want Martha and Lucy come back and take our jobs. But we took theirs. If I were them I'd probably hate every Irish person I saw. I wish it could all be different. I wish there were enough jobs for everybody. But a silver dollar and a fistful of pennies is all that stands between me and that newsboy who begs for scraps—between me and Blackwell's Island.

★★★

Later, when I'm out for Eliza's groceries, I find my way to Canal Street and the Bowery. As I ride downtown I hear newsboys calling out "Draft today!" and see clusters of folks talking in the street, all of them worn out with worry.

The theater has broad steps out front and seven great columns like a church. The sign over the door has a row of gaslights below it, and it says *Big Al's Variety Theater.* The door stands open and the sound of hammering comes from inside. On the front step in the sunlight, a man sits pumping the treadle of a sewing machine. He has gray hair and spectacles.

"Good morning," the man says to me. He peers over the top of his glasses. "Are you the golden songbird we have been watching for?"

"I think I am. Is Big Al here?"

"He'll be very happy to see you," the sewing man says.

I walk up the steps. There's something a bit familiar about his voice.

"I am Avrim," he says, leading the way inside.

"Avrim?" It's dimmer inside but I look him over more carefully. "Avrim the tailor?"

"Yes, of course, the tailor."

Inside it's a forest of scaffolding. Sawdust is thick on the floor. We walk down the middle aisle. A pair of black workers are bolting purple velvet chairs to the floor. They glance up as I go by and I recognize the one fellow, the bootblack, Samuel.

"Um—hello," I say to him awkwardly, hoping he won't remember me as the boy who tried to steal his work place.

Samuel looks up. "You again," he says sternly. "The hopping canary."

I duck my head for shame. "I'm sorry about that." I cut a glance his way but I can't guess what he's thinking.

"And you've come to audition for a dancing spot that isn't under the nose of a working man when he's trying to make a living?"

"I have," I say earnestly. "That's my entire plan."

"Good luck to you then." He turns back to his work.

The other carpenter gives me an encouraging nod. "Big Al is a fair-minded fellow, he says tilting his head toward the man on the stage. "You'll rise or fall on your merit alone, and that's a rare thing in this town."

"Thank you." If anyone would know the truth of that, it would be these two. I walk down the center aisle feeling a bit taller.

Halfway down the aisle, the ceiling soars up and balconies like the layers of a fantastical cake appear behind me. Two Italians on a scaffolding near the ceiling argue about the plasterwork. After two months of working with the maestro I can understand about every tenth word. Something about plaster and water and meatball sandwiches.

We stop in front of the stage. I never imagined it would be so big, nor the hall so fine. Avrim claps me on the shoulder.

"Take heart," he says. "This family has been good to me and kind. Took me in when I first came from Russia with nothing but a thimble to my name. I've made costumes for them ever since. Did you practice a song?"

I nod.

"Your voice will carry best if you stand in the middle of the stage. Do you need a sip of water?"

I shake my head. He gestures for me to go up on stage, but it suddenly seems much higher up than before and no place for an Irishman to be.

In a lowered area in front of the stage, three children sit and play a polka. A boy a little older than Kathleen is on the piano, a younger one is on the cello. A girl about my age plays the tiniest whistle

I have ever seen and she holds it off to the side her mouth instead of the front. All three of them have blue eyes and black hair. A fourth boy, much younger, peeks out from behind the piano and points at me.

The piano boy looks my way. "Dad! Hey, Dad!" he calls.

Big Al stands on the stage, intently watching a man in a violet top hat and matching tie who is juggling six balls at once. They fly in a circle at impossible speed, and then one by one he catches them, three to a hand, and bows with a great flourish. Behind him, a burly man in an undershirt and trousers throws knives of all shapes and sizes at a spinning target.

"Excellent, well done," Big Al says to the juggler. "But a ball this size is not easily seen from the balconies. Can you juggle something larger?"

"Yes, of course," the juggler says. "What do you prefer?"

"Anything big. Golden rings! Flaming torches!" Big Al says. "I want a blind man in the back row to see you plain as day."

"Dad!" the piano boy calls again.

Big Al turns. He sees me in the shadows, reaches his hands toward me, and gives me such a smile. In his smile I see a finished theater, every detail in perfect polish, the velvet curtain to match the chairs, the glow of gas lamps, the hush of a waiting audience. I feel a tug toward the stage like Kathleen feels the pull of a book. I don't belong here. I know I don't. But I want to belong.

"Here you are at last!" Big Al booms from the stage. "Come up! Come onstage."

Avrim gives me a gentle push and I walk up the steps like they are Jacob's Ladder. Big Al turns me around to look at the hundreds of empty seats in front of me. A chill goes up my spine.

"Picture this," Big Al says. "A full house. Not drunks, not loose women and gambling men. Families. Gentlefolk from every walk of life. And here."

Al gestures to the stage around us.

"Light! Music! Dancing! Sights to thrill the eye and sounds to lift the spirit. And you can be a part of it. Will you give it a try?"

I nod and Big Al waves the juggler and the knife thrower to the side. The stage feels like an entire acre of ground. I've always fit my steps into the smallest space I could—a hearthstone, a street corner, a crossroad.

I make a few bangs and clicks to warm up. The

stage boards ring out so much louder than pavement. Even better than the deck of a ship.

I turn to Big Al. "Is this allowed? Singing Irish songs? Won't they come take me away?"

"Of course not. You're in America now."

I pause for a moment and let that sink in. All my life I was shushed for singing where a stranger could hear me.

"Why would all those people want to hear an Irish boy? I'm not anyone."

"One quarter of all New Yorkers were born in Ireland. And many more are Irish by descent. They are going to pour through these doors every night, homesick, and hungry for what food won't give them. But you!" He puts a hand on my shoulder. "You can give them what money will never buy: comfort in a weary world and pride in all the troubles they've endured."

Big Al stands me in the center of the stage and then goes to stand in the middle aisle beside Avrim. "Sing something for me," he says.

"Something from your home," Avrim adds.

"Here's one about a girl who's the pride of her hometown." I take a deep breath, remembering everything the maestro taught me. I put my shoulders back and stand tall, remembering everything Packy taught me.

Near to Banbridge town in the County Down
One evening last July
Down a boreen green came a sweet colleen
And she smiled as she passed me by.

"The Star of the County Down" has a good swing to it, and a few bars in, the boy on the cello starts tapping a foot. By the second verse the piano has worked out a handful of chords.

When I finish out the final chorus I go straight into a reel. Last night I put a pair of short nails in the heel and toe of my old shoes. And a scrap of leather inside to keep them from poking me, just like the traveling dance masters do. As I stretch out the lead-around to fill up the stage I can hear the clicks and bangs echo off the back wall. I lift my hands up and beat time over my head until the band claps along. Then I launch into my right and left step. The carpenters leave off bolting the seats. The plasterers set down their trowels and brushes and lean over the scaffolding.

When I come to the end and make my bow, the

workers go straight back to their jobs without a murmur. But it doesn't matter. I can hear five hundred people cheering.

"I knew you could do it," Big Al says quietly, coming back on the stage. He gestures for the juggler and knife thrower to go back to practicing. "Let's get your parents and make a contract."

I feel a squeeze of panic. The barred windows of an orphan asylum swim into my imagination. People go to Blackwell's Island but you never hear of them coming back. I can't let him know I'm the last of the name. Kathleen would never forgive me.

"It's the middle of the day. They're working." I look for the door and inch away from him.

"Hold on. What is it? Margaret Fortino! Come see to this child!"

A woman with a baby on one hip and a little boy trailing after comes out of the wings. "What's the trouble, lad? Don't you have parents?"

She and Big Al stand between me and the way out.

"He must," Big Al insists. "Look how clean he is. And he's no thief. I tempted him to take the harmonica player's cash already. Wouldn't take a penny more than his due."

"Why else would he be afraid?" Mrs. Fortino says. "He wasn't afraid a minute ago when he was dancing."

"Someone must be protecting him," Avrim says. "The clothes are clean and mended. There's no smell of the streets on him. Do you think he could spend his days eating garbage and then dance like he did?"

"Come now, Daniel," Big Al says. "We want to help you. We can give you a job and a home if you need it."

"It's my sister I live with," I blurt out. "We're all that's left."

Mrs. Fortino gives the baby to Big Al. She puts both hands on my shoulders. "There's no shame in that. Won't she be proud of you when she hears you've got a proper job?"

I shake my head vigorously. "She's fearful strict. Doesn't hold with theater at all."

"Good for her!" Mrs. Fortino says. "Up till now she'd be right. The theater was no place for respectable people."

"But we're going to change all that," Al says. "Bring her to us and we'll show her. Let her meet my family."

He hands the baby back to Mrs. Fortino. "This

one is Angelo. Vincent and Anthony are the twins," he says, pointing to the boy hiding behind his wife and the other one hiding behind the piano. "And then we have Alberto Jr., the piano; Paolo, the cello; and of course my Bianca, the piccolo."

"Plenty of room around our table for you," Mrs. Fortino says. "Come eat with us."

"No, I have to get back. They'll miss me."

"You have a job here," Al insists. "What do they pay you where you work now? Fifty cents a week? A dollar? I will pay you a dollar a show. Five shows a week and two on Saturday."

My heart skips a beat. I could send Kathleen to college. We could have a home. I can persuade her. I will.

"And Sundays will be your own," Mrs. Fortino adds with a smile. "To do with as you will."

"Or as my sister wills?"

"That's what I was thinking." Mrs. Fortino winks. "She's a girl after the Sunday Mass unless I miss my guess."

"She is."

"And how would you like to take that sister to church in a carriage of your own? You'll be able to soon enough."

I picture Kathleen with a bundle of schoolbooks under her arm and the halls of college before her.

"I'll do it," I say. "May I bring her on Sunday?"

"We'll be waiting. Let's get you a cab home."

***

On the way back to the Treadwell house, traffic slows to a stop around the armory. The double doors are thrown open. A great wooden drum, six feet tall, stands on a riser with a uniformed officer turning it. Another officer with a megaphone and a corporal with a pen and paper stand at the ready to copy down the names of the men drafted. A crowd of a hundred working men and women stands outside, and when the lunch bell rings in the factory across the street, more workers pour out to join the throng.

The driver gets out of the cab to calm his horse and lead him through the crowd. The drum full of names stops turning and the officer opens a little door and fishes out a slip of paper.

"Michael Sullivan!" the officer shouts through his trumpet. Grumblings of anger pass through the crowd. The driver talks softly to the horse and inches him forward. As we move on, the chorus of names grows softer in the distance.

"Gavin O'Toole, Gustav Sorenson, Kevin Murphy, John Kelly, Joseph Kennedy, Angelo Verdi, Finn McCann, Conner O'Brien."

You don't have to be a mathematical genius to hear that more than a quarter of those names called are Irish.

THE IMPENDING BATTLEFIELD:
Scene of the Present Movements and
Operations of the Contending Armies . . .

—*New York Herald*

CHAPTER 17

The whole way home, I am bursting with the news about my audition. A real contract! A dollar a show! It'll be the making of us.

I scramble back into the dress and run for the back door still tying on my apron. Kathleen is not in the kitchen. I snatch the usual afternoon roll from the cooling rack and get the usual whack on the ear from Cook's wooden spoon. I dash up the stairs before Cook has even begun her lengthy description of my poor character and dodgy prospects.

Kathleen isn't in the parlor or the music room or the study or the dining room. I finally find her at the top of the house, stripped down to her slip and sweating like a racehorse as she hems and tucks and fusses over the peach colored satin dress Mrs. Treadwell finally pronounced adequate for the soirée.

I know better than to fret her with my news. I grab a spare needle and we work silently side by side until it's too dark to see the stitches.

***

Saturday is hotter. Kathleen's already up and working when I wake at sunrise. A wagonload of food is delivered and Cook throws half of it out for spoilage. She sends for the iceman, but he doesn't come. She sends Reeve after more groceries and he's gone for hours. The entire block can hear Mrs. Treadwell yelling at the piano tuner.

It's hours past lunch when I finally catch Kathleen on the back stairs. "I have news. It's important!"

"It can wait," she says grimly, putting one exhausted foot in front of the other.

"It's good news!" I call after her as she disappears upstairs.

I head out to the back to take laundry off the line, just in time to see Alice from across the alley slip out of her gate. I don't blame her one bit.

They're drawing names for the draft again. She has four brothers in that big wooden drum and a father already on the battlefield.

Eliza watches her go and, without a word, grabs her cane and hobbles over to the yard across the way to fold her laundry. I finish hanging up mine and join her. Bridget from the other side brings over a jam jar full of cornflowers. Eliza kisses her on the cheek. There's nothing to say. We've all lost brothers. We thought that America would be the end of war for us, not the beginning.

★★★

Sunday is even hotter still. I watered Cook's prized lettuces in the kitchen garden twice yesterday, and they are flat in the dirt this morning to spite me. Mrs. Treadwell fumes as we go off to church, but Kathleen resolutely marches me out the back door. There isn't a speck of breeze or cooling dew. The pavement is still hot from yesterday. I take note of the weary set of Kathleen's shoulders. She needs good news.

"Do you remember how Mother Hildegard said we should keep looking for a better job?" I begin.

"I do."

We are walking past the cathedral construction site and more than a dozen women are swarming over the site collecting scraps of stone in their aprons. It's odd. Children scavenge in the streets for coal all the time. I never see women doing it. And why would they need stones?

"I've found a job. A good job with a decent employer." I glance at Kathleen sidelong and decide that in this mood of hers a little buttering up it in order. "Naturally I told him I couldn't consent to a job without my mother's blessing." I beam a great smile at her.

"Did you, now," she answers, not even looking at me.

A cluster of men across the way have caught her eye. They have a city map among them and are arguing about where the police have their stations and which is the closest armory and what kind of guns are inside it.

We round the corner only to find the barbershop open and packed with men. Only this time, it's not the barber singing. In fact Matteo is nowhere in sight. It's a tall and sunburned Irishman with a blackthorn stick in his hand singing out "By The Rising of the Moon"—the old call to arms. It tells the story of the battle of '98, the one that took Da's grandpa and all his uncles in one day.

Now come tell me Sean O'Farrell
Where the gathering is to be
At the old spot by the river
Quite well known to you and me
One more word for signal token
Whistle up the marching tune
With your pike upon your shoulder
At the rising of the moon.

Bottles pass among the singing men. They are gray-haired, the lot of them. Already given up a son or two to the Irish Brigade. Maybe lost a son or two back in Ireland. And here comes Lincoln hunting after more of their sons. They've got the green flag with the gold harp—the standard of the Irish Brigade—draped out over the mirror. A fellow reaches out to stroke the tattered fringe at the flag's edge as you'd stroke the cheek of a child. It's proud they are of their boys, even in their grief. More men join in on the following verses. It becomes more of a shouting session than a song.

All along that singing river
That great mass of men was seen
High above their shining weapons
Flew their own beloved green
Death to every foe and traitor!
Whistle up the marching tune
And hurrah, me boys, for freedom!
'Tis the rising of the moon.

The leader of the song circles the singing men back to the beginning, leaving out the last verse, the one my father could never sing without a tear in his eye.

And they fought for poor old Ireland
And full bitter was their fate,
Oh what glorious pride and sorrow
Fills the names of '98.
Yet thank God, e'en still are beating
Hearts in manhood burning noon,
Who would follow in their footsteps
At the rising of the moon.

"Drinking at this hour," Kathleen says in disgust. She pulls me along and I feel the shaking of her hands.

A few blocks farther and it's a group of women clustered around a newspaper.

"Look, it says right here, you can buy your way out of the draft for three hundred dollars," a woman with a baby in arms says.

"As if there's a one of us with ready cash in such amounts," chimes in another. "Why that's a year's wage."

"The disgrace of it!" a third woman shouts. "Three hundred dollars! A slave is worth a thousand!"

"Who is this Lincoln to count our lives so cheaply?"

"They'll take our vote next. See if they don't. Black men can't vote but they're worth a thousand! Who would give a vote to a man only worth three hundred?"

Kathleen hustles me into church but it's not better inside. I hear whispers all down the pew. Such a cloud of discontent is over the parish that only a few stragglers come to the dinner downstairs afterward.

Mother Hildegard presides over the food. She takes a whole loaf of the soda bread and wraps it in a cloth.

"Take this now and get thee indoors," she says. "It's not a fit day for young ones to be abroad in the street."

Out on the church steps, I try to get Kathleen to sit down and listen to me. She's not having it. Not after Mother Hildegard's warning. All my best pleading sheets off of her like rain.

At first I drag behind her on the way uptown. But then clouds roll in thick and black. I look for the relief of rain, but there is not one breath of wind. The street corners are silent now and the barber-shop empty. I see a black man flit from one shadowy alley to the next, a traveling bag in his hand. A block farther on and I see a whole black family running toward the railway station just as the cars pull in. The entire train is full of black families, ducking down so they won't be seen from the windows and traveling in complete silence.

Clouds cover the city like the lid of a pot. I feel a flash of sympathy for lobsters.

The farther north we go the more we see homes of the wealthy with windows boarded over as you would for a great storm. I see men with rifles on rooftops. The last bits of blue sky vanish and an eerie yellow light falls over the streets. Hanging weather, Granny used to call it. I never asked her why.

CHAPTER 18

MONDAY, JULY 13, 1863

On the morning of the grand soirée, I stand in Valor's room, surveying my costume with revulsion—layers of blue silk over layers of muslin over a cage of hoops such as you might keep a wild beast in. To compensate for all the weight below, there's no sleeve to speak of and a swooping low neck that Mrs. Vanderzanden called daring when Mrs. Treadwell made me try it on for her approval. She's the monster who told the lady of the house that my freckles needed to be plastered over with a pot of what looks and smells like wallpaper paste. I pace the room.

"It's just a costume," I say to Valor's baseball bat in the corner. "Kathleen will come help me. She'll make it bearable." I have a great dread that Mrs. Treadwell will bust into the room and dress me herself.

The clock ticks on. Yesterday's clouds are still thick over the rooftops. I lift the window, hoping for a breeze. In the street, I see three carriages careening by at top speed. Elegant ladies cling to their children. Gentlemen hold fast to baggage. Coachmen whip the horses to a lather.

What on earth?

On the sidewalk, four stout women march downtown. In their well-calloused hands they hold a rolling pin, a pry bar, a cartwheel wrench, and a fireplace poker. A ragged boy with a note in hand rings the front bell and runs off leaving the note under the mat.

I hurry down the servant's stairs, still in the maid's dress, to look for Kathleen. On the way around a blind corner at top speed, I run smack into Eliza. I gasp in shock. I can't imagine going into any of the great houses on the block. I feel like a thief just thinking of it.

Eliza grabs my arm to steady me and pulls in close to whisper. "It's gone you must be. The mob is coming. They're in a burning mood."

"Mob?"

"Men called up for the draft." She goes on, "They got angry, broke the wheel, and burned the draft records. You'd think that would satisfy them but then they went to the armory and stole weapons. They're coming after the three-hundred-dollar men. They chopped down the telegraph lines so the police won't be able to message where the mob is. They've gone wild. Thousands of them."

I stand bewildered. She pushes a bundle of Michael's clothes into my arms and then cups my face in her hands.

"Go as yourself, Daniel. Go swiftly. And angels carry you."

She kisses me once on the brow and is gone. I don't need more encouragement. I sprint for the attic.

Kathleen is already there. She's taken off her uniform and put on the old homespun.

"Hurry!" she says breathlessly. "There's a mob—"

"—I heard."

"They have torches, Danny. Torches!" The memory of our burning cottage and fields flashes before us both.

Kathleen has our clothes packed. She drags the

old bundle with Granny's treasure out from under the bed. I tear off the maid's dress without waiting for her to turn her back and pull on the pants and shirt Eliza gave me. Kathleen gets our wages from under the floorboard. It's almost four dollars. A fortune compared to the three pennies we had when we arrived. I grab the dancing money from its hiding place while Kathleen strips the bed and presses the blanket Mrs. Treadwell took from our wages into our traveling case.

"We'll go to Mother Hildegard," Kathleen says. "She'll give us shelter and good counsel."

I don't argue. It's halfway to Big Al's theater. I'll get Kathleen there yet. I even feel a little thrill of adventure now that pants are snug around me.

I hear the clang of a fire bell and smell the first whiff of smoke. A few more Bridgets and a butler or two are running toward the trouble. A boy in rags runs the other direction with a gleaming silver candlestick in each hand.

"Ready?"

"God help us," Kathleen replies.

Mrs. Treadwell is waiting for us at the bottom of the servants' stairs. The stair is so narrow there is absolutely no way to pass her.

"And where do you little thieves imagine you are going?"

There's a wild look in her eye. She's dressed for the soirée in all her satins and jewels.

Temperance is right behind, in her finery, hair ribbons in hand. She glares at Kathleen. "My hair. You haven't finished dressing my hair."

Every inch of the marble front hall gleams. Reeve spent hours lining up the chairs in the music room yesterday. Even the chandeliers are clean.

Nobody is coming. Not today.

There's a great rumbling of wagons in the street. All four of us rush to the window. Temperance screams when she sees a woman in a wagon outside. She has one arm around a man who is bleeding from the head and the other on the reins of a horse in full panic. Mrs. Treadwell takes Kathleen by the arm and drags her into the front parlor. I trail after them looking for something I can use as a weapon.

There is no whiff of breakfast from downstairs, nor sound of Sophia setting the long table with the finest china. The butler's station is vacant. Kathleen takes it in with a glance and gives me a warning nod.

"We've come for you," she lies boldly. "In disguise of course," she adds, pointing to my pants and shirt. "I have a dress for you here." She hands our case to Temperance. "A maid's dress. That and a simple braid in your hair and you could be any Colleen from the Bowery."

Kathleen turns to Mrs. Treadwell. "Have the others gone?"

The lady of the house is one knot of fury. She can't even speak.

"Go to Cook's room and take whatever clothing she left," Kathleen says firmly. "Or if there's nothing, take off the petticoats and tie an apron over what you're wearing. Leave the earrings behind and put on a work cap."

Mrs. Treadwell stands as dumbfounded as Temperance.

"Ladies, please," Kathleen says. "An angry mob of drafted men has formed in the Five Points. They've taken weapons from the armory. They are beating every rich man they find. They are burning houses!"

"But why?" Temperance wails. "It's not our fault they got drafted. We had nothing to do with it. We don't even like Lincoln!"

"Do you think they care?" I snap. "They'd rather fight and die on their home ground than go die in a war not their own."

Mrs. Treadwell takes Kathleen's arm and twists it behind her back. "What's your plan then, you thief? We leave with you and then you lead us to the mob?"

I move to step between them, but Kathleen lunges forward and slips out of her grasp. She turns and speaks like you would to a dullard. "This house is the magnet," she says. "Once we are gone from it, we can blend in with the crowds and make our way north. The docks are swarming with longshoremen still angry about the strike breakers. I can see from the upstairs window that the ferryboats have all left and they aren't coming back. The railway in Harlem is our best shot at getting out of the city."

The two women lock eyes. Kathleen stands tall and in that moment she is mighty Oisin and fearsome Finn McCool and the great pirate queen Grace O'Malley all rolled into one. No wonder Mrs. Treadwell backs down.

"A disguise," Kathleen says to her. "Quickly."

Mrs. Treadwell heads for the kitchen and Kathleen disappears with Temperance to help her change but mostly to keep her from screaming again. I have a moment alone in the parlor.

I go to the piano and play a single note. My heart aches as the sweet tone of it fills the room. Empty chairs face me. My grand debut. I would have loved to learn the piano. Temperance's warm-up piece, "Beautiful Dreamer," is on the piano stand. On impulse I hide it under my shirt for her.

"I am not carrying a suitcase full of books forty blocks to the train station," Kathleen says. She marches resolutely down the hall, Temperance trailing after her in a maid's dress, apron and all.

"But—but—it's poetry!"

I decide to keep the music for myself.

"I am not your maid now," Kathleen says.

Mrs. Treadwell comes up the stairs in a cook's apron and cap. "No jewels," Kathleen says firmly.

"I won't leave my rubies to be stolen. They're mine. Mine, and I'll have them."

"Are those jewels worth more than your life? More than your daughter's life?"

With much grumbling Mrs. Treadwell takes off her necklace and earrings and hides them. She heads for the front door.

"Servants use the back," I say. It thrills me far more than it should when the lady of the house does what I say.

Kathleen puts her hands on her hips and gives the ladies of the house a stern look. "Heads down.

Look meek. And whatever you do don't speak aloud. Those American accents will give you away in a heartbeat."

We charge down the back stair and into the alley. Everyone is gone from the block except Eliza. She has taken off her uniform but she paces the backyard with her hands on a rosary and her eyes on heaven.

"Come away with us!" I call to her.

"How will my Michael ever find me if I go?" she answers. "I promised him I'd always be here."

We run up the alley, but I look over my shoulder for Eliza long after she's fallen from sight. The air is thick with smoke now and I can hear chanting, and the clang of fire bells and the whistle of coppers all heading downtown.

"Through the park," Mrs. Treadwell hisses through clenched teeth. "It's a shortcut."

"We're safer in the alleys," I say.

"They're full of servants," Temperance whisper-shouts.

"We are servants!" Kathleen shushes her as the next group of cooks and maids runs past, heading for the thick of the trouble.

We work our way north, past Hamilton Square, up into the seventies and then the eighties. I lift up the hair from my sweaty neck. A gritty snow of ash sweeps along with the wind, and the smell of burning, and the deep boom of things exploding.

"Oh, we're done for," Mrs. Treadwell mutters. "The dirty Irish. We should have kept them out while we had the chance."

"I have to sit down," Temperance whimpers. "I'm so sweaty. And this vile dress itches."

Kathleen urges them on a few blocks more, but it's clear they're not used to being up on their feet. Mrs. Treadwell insists we go find a bench in the park. The two of them collapse on it and fall to waving their faces with their aprons. Kathleen and I take a few steps away from them.

"What's your plan?" I whisper.

"We just have to get them on a train."

"And then what?"

"We still have our treasure," she says lightly. "Granny always said it would save us."

"Are you ever going to tell me what's in that bundle?"

"Better you don't know. Safer."

I fall to imagining a fairy contained in a box who will break out and shower us with gold at just the right moment.

A wagon with a well-dressed woman and five wailing children careens up the street. An old man and a younger one in top hats and velvet jackets follow them in a buggy. A tall fellow in work clothes springs out of the shrubbery. Four other toughs follow him. The big one rushes in front of the horse waving a rag in each hand. The horse swerves left and then back, but the man dodges in front of her each time until she comes to a stop. And then he's all soothing words and holding her still by the bridle.

"You there!" the older man in the carriage shouts. "Turn my horse loose!"

The other toughs grab him by the collar and drag him onto the sidewalk right in front of the Treadwells. A shock of recognition flashes over Mrs. Treadwell's face. Kathleen grabs Temperance by the hand and pulls her away. She clamps a hand over her mouth in case she's stupid enough to say the man's name out loud. I try to pull Mrs. Treadwell away, too, but she is rooted to the spot in horrified fascination.

"What have we here?" the leader of the toughs says once the pair of gentlemen are wrestled to the ground. "A rich man and his able-bodied son, fleeing the service of their country."

"Well that's not right."

"Shameful."

One of them has a blackthorn stick and the rest hold crowbars and metal pipe.

"How many months have you served your country in arms?"

"Have you lost an arm or a leg in service?"

"How many sons have you lost?"

The gentlemen look from one soot-smeared face to another.

"N-n-none," the older stammers.

"Did you think we wouldn't notice?" says the one with the pipe. "Did you think a war would come and you'd never have to pay the butcher's bill?"

"Our lot, we've paid our share already. Paid in blood!"

"Perhaps you're feeling the urge to volunteer now."

"No? Maybe you'll just pay the three hundred for each of us then, since we've no desire to be drafted either."

"We d-don't have it. No one carries so much ready money." The younger gentleman strains to get away, but he's no match for men who make their living on the docks.

"Strip them down!" the man holding the horse says. "We'll find what they're made of."

One of them walks up to Mrs. Treadwell where she sits frozen on the park bench. He leans into her.

"You might want to run along, like. This next bit won't be pretty."

She hops up and hurries away with her hands clamped over her ears so she can't hear the screaming. I hear every scream, and the sickening thud of metal against flesh and the moans that follow after, when a man has suffered past all screaming.

We run back to the alleys and although there is much huffing and puffing from Mrs. Treadwell and Temperance and even some unladylike nose wiping and scratching, they leave off the complaining. Houses become fewer and gardens much bigger as we get to Harlem. At last the train station is ahead. There's a steam train ready to go, the one o'clock to Hartford.

"Oh, thank God," Temperance gasps as we burst into the station.

It's crowded with upper-crust folk. Mrs. Treadwell stands in line for a ticket. Temperance totters over to the bench, but not a single gentleman there will rise to give her a seat, dressed as she is in a maid's uniform and smelling exactly like she's just run forty blocks.

"Two tickets to Hartford," Mrs. Treadwell says to the man in the ticket booth.

"A dollar and forty cents."

She draws a long slip of paper from her sleeve. "May I trouble you for a pen?"

"We do not accept checks."

"Don't be ridiculous! The man before me paid with a check."

"Of course. A man. You must have your husband with you to cosign the check and then we will gladly accept it."

"My husband is in Montana, you blockhead!"

"A registered letter in your husband's own hand authorizing this transaction would be acceptable."

"A letter takes a month!"

Mrs. Treadwell takes a deep breath and smooths out the blank check before her.

"I use credit on Mr. Treadwell's account all the time. How do you think we manage a household while he's gone? I'm sure we can come to some accommodation. Perhaps you would suggest a processing fee and sign in his stead?"

The ticket agent gives her an appraising look from her cook's cap to her un-calloused fingers. "These regulations exist to keep wives from abandoning

their husbands and unscrupulous servants from rob-
bing their masters." His full beard and whiskers
quiver with indignation. "God defend us from the
day women ever get control of their husbands' bank
accounts. It will be the end of marriage!"

He slides the ticket window shut with a snap.

Mrs. Treadwell stands frozen for a moment, but
then she turns to me and Kathleen with her usual
brisk tone.

"Change of plans!"

She motions us to follow her and we do. Out of
habit I suppose. As soon as we are out of sight of the
station windows she grabs hold of my hair, whips a
kitchen knife out of her pocket and holds it fast to
my throat.

"Give me your money!" she growls to Kathleen.

"What money?" I strain and squirm against her.

"Your wages. I hear it in your sister's pocket. Jin-
gling away these last forty-three blocks."

"Take it," Kathleen says frantically. She pulls
the handkerchief full of coins out of her pocket.
She throws it to the ground at my feet and when
Mrs. Treadwell reaches for it, she grabs my shirtfront
and pulls me free. Mrs. Treadwell scoops up all our
wages, and when Kathleen leans over to put her arms

246

around me, Mrs. Treadwell takes hold of the bundle on Kathleen's back.

"And I'll take this treasure you've been whispering about behind my back." She gives the bundle a good yank.

"You'll not have it!" Kathleen snarls.

"You thief! You common thug! What have you stolen from my house?"

Mrs. Treadwell tugs harder and the bag tears asunder.

A harp tumbles to the ground with a hollow thud—a small harp, bowed in the front and flat in the back with a smooth curve of wood along the top. It's black and dusty and a few of the strings are missing. Kathleen gasps and snatches it up to her heart with a sob.

"Is that your treasure? You pathetic thing!"

And with that Mrs. Treadwell turns on her heel and leaves to the piercing shriek of the train whistle.

CHAPTER 19

MONDAY, JULY 13, 1863

The train pulls away with great whooshes of steam. Kathleen sits in the dead grass behind the station, cradling the harp in her lap and fighting back tears. I hear a bee, a fat and fuzzy bumblebee, going from one wilted dandelion to another. Down the block is a house, a pump, and long rows of vegetables. Along the next block is a row of houses being built. Beyond them are the fields and trees of Harlem. I feel as small and alone as I did fresh from the ocean crossing. No food, no roof. Four months of wages, gone in a heartbeat.

"Is it broken?" I say at last.

She runs her fingers over the harp's soundboard. She checks the joining at the neck.

I have always wanted an instrument of my own. Da took his tin whistle to Australia. It was the only thing of comfort we had to give him. There used to be a man in the village with a bodhrán and he'd beat time for dancers on it. There used to be a fiddler before the Great Hunger.

The harp was everywhere in Granny's stories. Chief Dagda of old had a harp and the evil Formorians stole it from him. Loads of adventure to win it back. A harp is on the Irish Brigade's flag, it's on the old Irish coins, but I've never seen a real one before. I reach a finger toward the strings. Kathleen pulls it away.

"I promised Granny I'd keep it a secret. She made me swear to keep it safe. She said it has a power. She said it could save our lives."

"How?"

"She didn't say."

"You didn't ask her? How could you not ask her about something that could save our lives?"

"I did. I begged her. She died."

Kathleen seems old to me, much older than sixteen. But now that I look at her, really look, sixteen is young.

Kathleen gets out a needle. You'd think now that the Treadwells are gone, she'd never want to sew again.

"Why should a harp with missing strings be a secret?" I say.

Kathleen smooths out the torn canvas sack that has carried the harp so long. She takes thread from her case and gets to work on a repair. I'm so tired of running that I'm content to sit in the shade beside her and watch grasshoppers and ladybugs.

"It belonged to Da's people—generations back," Kathleen says at last. "Da didn't like to speak of it."

Kathleen looks all around to see that we're alone.

"He was a famous harper. Pride of the county. Not a hall that wouldn't receive him. The old princes of Ireland loved him and gave him their patronage and he wrote songs for them and carried the news from one court to the next. There was nobody a prince respected more than a harper."

"What happened?"

"That bloody-minded Queen Elizabeth, she hated the Irish and our harpers most of all."

"What for?"

"She wanted our country, plain and simple, and we fought her for it. She sent her soldiers to cut off the fingers of any man caught with a harp. She knew what would hurt us most."

On instinct I curl my fingers up tight and hide my hands under my shirt. The English are more about cutting off ears these days. Still, the thought of a fingerless harper fills me with horror. The ancient harpers from the old stories—most of them were blind men. It's one thing for a Queen to give a command from her glittering throne across the sea. Some man of hers had to actually do the deed—look a blind man in the face, his family wailing all around him, and cut off all his fingers.

"Plenty died of those wounds, but our man lived. He disguised himself as a beggar when he traveled, and he taught the harp in secret."

"Like the hedge master with the reading and writing?"

"Just so. But then at the end of her reign and the height of her great cruelty the dark Queen gave the order: Burn every harp and hang every harper."

I pull my knees up to my chest. It happened more than two hundred years ago. Why does it hit me so fresh? Kathleen is still hunched over her sewing, eyes fixed on the needle, and also on the long ragged thread of our history.

"They hung him then?"

"In front of a bonfire of instruments: harps, pipes, fiddles, and drums. They say the heart went out of all Ireland in those days. We were never the same since."

I have seen enough cottages set to the torch to imagine this bonfire. I hate fire. Maybe even more than hunger. No, it's the police; I hate them the most. Now that I've opened the door, the ocean of things I hate washes over me like the driving rains that come out of the North Atlantic in the winter. I hate the poorhouse. I hate the courts that never give an Irishman a fair hearing. I hate the snitch who turned Da in for trying to feed us when we were starving. I hate the landlord who turned us out for no cause. I hate the captain who watched a hundred hungry people board his ship and didn't provide food enough for the passage. I hate Reeve who stole the wages we worked for. I hate the fear of being hungry. And I hate, hate, hate more than anything that we are alone in the world with no hearth of our own to gather around. I am full to bursting with memory and nobody to share out the burden of remembering.

I could drown in all this hating.

Kathleen takes me by the hand. "Not every harp," she says. "This one was hidden, under the thatch of our cottage roof. And before that buried. Sealed up in a cave. Carted from one hiding place to another under a load of peat or potatoes, by folk who risked their lives to keep it secret. You're from brave people. Don't ever forget it."

"Liars and scoff-laws from the sound of it," I say, feeling not so bad about the lying I've done in this light.

"Seekers of trouble," Kathleen says with a sly smile. "Drawn to it like a compass needle to the north."

"The good trouble, Granny used to call it." I stand up, stretch my weary shoulders, and look to the south where black smoke is rising up from the city to the black storm clouds above. "What kind of trouble do you think they've got down there in the Five Points?"

"All trouble looks bad from the outside. I guess we'll know what kind when we're in it."

"Are you ready?" I reach out a hand and haul her to her feet.

"Here's something that doesn't jingle in the pocket," she says and pulls a potato out of her apron.

There was a bowl of yesterday's potatoes on the kitchen sideboard to be made into hash this morning. She must have snatched one on the way out the door. I break it in half and hold out the two pieces for her to pick. She always picks the smaller one and when I was little I'd take shameless advantage. But she sees I've done an even job of the breaking, and knowing that she sees it fills me up a little bit even before eating.

CHAPTER 20

We turn south, eating slow and walking slower. It's the hottest part of the afternoon and we have miles to go. No one is out but us. Not a soul working the gardens, nor a supply wagon going down the Old Post Road. A dozen blocks on and we come to the first of the construction sites for new houses. As we walk we can see three and then five and then nine different columns of smoke. The sound of the mob is so much like thunder from a mile away that I keep expecting rain to fall.

"We'll go to Mother Hildegard," Kathleen says firmly. "She won't turn us out."

I put my hand to my pocket. My dancing money is there, every penny of it. There's never going to be a better time to tell her.

"So," I say, crossing both fingers and spitting over my shoulder for luck. "Since you've had me lying about being a girl it's led to a great degeneration of my moral character. I've become quite the desperate sinner to honest."

She looks at me sharpish but keeps walking.

"I've been doing Eliza's marketing for her. You know how her leg hurts her. So she loaned me her son's clothes. I just couldn't bear pretending all the time. I felt like I was losing myself and all my brothers, too."

Kathleen doesn't say anything but she puts an arm over my shoulder and keeps walking.

"Well, once I was out there as myself, I made friends at the market—Mr. Ryan, the greengrocer, and Matteo, the barber—and I met this old soldier. A wounded fellow with a mouth organ that he plays for tips."

I cast a sidelong glance as we walk. So far, Kathleen shows no sign of wanting to murder me.

"I heard him play, and I just had to stop and listen. And then he was playing a song I knew and I couldn't stop myself from singing. And then the most amazing thing happened."

I pause for dramatic effect.

"A man gave me a penny."

"A what?"

"A penny, just like that. For no reason but the song. And then another man gave me another penny and more pennies after that."

Kathleen stops. She folds her arms and purses her lips. My heart starts pounding but I press on, God help me.

"And then a crowd gathered. Some fellow in the back shouted out, *Jig it, laddie!* And what could I do?"

"You danced?" Kathleen says. "In *public*?"

"I did. I'm sorry! I know you don't hold with dancing in front of men. But it wasn't like that. I swear. Nobody hurt me. I promise."

"And they gave you money?" Kathleen is completely dumbfounded.

"They did." I pause for breath, astonished that she hasn't clouted me over the head so far. "But it's more than that. They thanked me, with real kindness. Not one of them scorned my way of speech. Nobody told me I was dirty or shameful. They stopped for a minute in their working day and just listened. I like the money and I know we need it. But it lifted their hearts too and . . . and . . ."

I reach for Kathleen's hand, but she stands aloof with a look of shock on her face. I throw my arms around her middle and lean my head on her shoulder. "I like making people happy. I was proud of the dances I know. I've never been proud before." I look up at Kathleen. "I'll stop if you make me, but please, *please* don't make me."

Kathleen untangles herself from me. She takes me by both shoulders and looks me hard in the face.

"They gave you money?" she says again.

I dig into my pocket and take out the rag that's knotted around my pennies and nickels. I hold it in my palm and give it a jingle. "Two dollars and thirty-seven cents."

Her eyes go wide and her face goes pale. "You did this all by yourself? You? You!"

I brace for impact.

"Ye brilliant boyo!" She scoops me up in a hug that near to cracks my ribs. "You!" She gives me another squeeze. "Wouldn't Packy be proud? All those dances he loved so well!"

She sets me down but I'm still dizzy.

"One more thing," I say. I take Big Al's silver dollar out of my shoe where I've been hiding it. "I met a man who owns a theater."

Kathleen looks at the silver dollar, mesmerized, and I pour out the whole story of Big Al and his offer of a job. I beg her to let me take it, but only a little. I can see she's worn out with worry. I don't blame her. I was worried myself before I went to his theater and met his family. In the end, she agrees to think about it and I agree to go to Mother Hildegard's first and ask her advice. She seems to know everyone under the sun. If Big Al is really a bad man and only pretending to be my friend, she'll warn us.

We come to the top of the park. By the pond there are rows of tents for the invalid soldier's unit but they all stand empty. The grand houses on the east side of the park stand just as empty. It's spooky to see the city so quiet, and not know exactly where the mob has gone. There aren't any newsboys this far north to shout the headlines. If it weren't for the smoke in the air I'd think everyone had left town.

I take off my shoes, roll up my pants and dip my feet in the pond. Sweet relief! Kathleen looks at me with undisguised envy and fans her face with her apron.

"Do you suppose we could find a job where I could dress as a boy for a change?" Kathleen says.

"Well, how do you feel about hod carrying?" I pantomime the wide platform a hod carrier puts on his shoulders and stagger under a pretend weight of bricks.

"Do you remember the soggy rat-infested hold on the ship?"

Kathleen shudders.

"You could be one of them longshoremen that carries the cargo out of the hold."

I splash her and she leans into the relief of cool water.

"Or a carter! Who hauls horse manure off the streets the livelong day."

She glares at me.

"I hear from the butcher that a man can make a good living as a prizefighter if he isn't so attached to the right shape of his nose."

I start getting a little nervous about the shape of my own nose but I can't resist. And she can't box my ears from an arm's length away and knee deep in the pond.

"It's not that I'd mind sharing, but I don't think my pants would fit you."

"That's it, little man!" Kathleen cries. She tugs off her apron. Drenches it in one swoop of her arm. I like my odds less and less. I turn and start running through the water, but not fast enough. Her wet apron snakes out and snaps me across the back of the neck. Fair play to her. I had that one coming.

Refreshed, we walk through the trees. We head for Fifth Avenue, chatting at first but then falling quiet as the great houses along the avenue come into view. The mob is long gone, the streets empty, but everywhere we look, broken windows look back. Doors swing crooked on their hinges. A few are burned, but you can look in the gaping doors and see that everything inside is gone, from grand paintings and draperies to chairs and carpets.

"You there!" a policeman shouts.

We scramble for a spot to hide but there's nothing left on the street. The very lampposts are bent to the ground or snapped off entirely. The only possible shelter is an upturned hansom cab, its dead horse still in the traces.

"Are you mad, the pair of you? Wandering the streets with a mob out!" the policeman says. His face is smudged with soot and his eyes have the look of a fellow who's stayed up all night and seen horrors beyond description.

"We're going home, sir." Kathleen says. "Only a few more blocks."

"What happened?" I can't help asking.

"'Tis wild they've gone," the copper says. "At first it was just the draft names they were after.

They broke the draft wheel and scattered the names in the street. But then they came after the three-hundred-dollar men. Throwing bricks and bottles. Burning houses. Stealing guns and powder from the armory."

"Where are they now?"

"There's talk of lynching the mayor and more talk of burning the newspaper offices. So they're well south of here. Down in the Bowery by now, I reckon."

I get a lump in my throat thinking about Big Al's theater.

"Take your sister straight home, do you hear me? And steer clear of the waterfront. Them longshoremen are in a rage—beating black men, and burning pubs if you can imagine such a thing. It's bedlam at the docks to be sure. If your home is on fire, come to the station on Mulberry Street. We'll take you in."

"Thank you," Kathleen says, as amazed as me to see a policeman with a care for the common man.

We press on, and the roar and snap of fire grows louder with every step. A baker's shop is completely cleaned out. Nothing but crumbs. A barber shop, untouched. The college is as serene as ever behind its curling ironwork gates, but the Colored Orphans Asylum on Fourty-Third is on fire, every window broken. The orphans are gone. On the sidewalk outside I see a lone child's sock twisted and trampled.

Where will they go now that their fine house is in cinders? I push away the memory of iron bars and damp blankets and filth. Wherever they end up, I hope it's not Blackwell's Island.

A fire truck is on hand. It's the one with the snarling tiger painted on the tank. I look for the firemen who greeted us so kindly on our first day in New York. Only four men work the pump where there should be ten. Kathleen looks too, a tear welling up as she searches their faces. The men are so exhausted, and covered in soot that they look as if they've walked up out of a grave.

We hustle along. The fire roars and snaps on both sides of the street. Folks run every which way. Kathleen screams when flames jump the narrow alleyways from one building to the next right in front of us. Another fire truck runs past, wounded men and women hanging off the sides.

"*Faugh a ballagh*," The fireman bellows from the front of the fire truck—the old battle call: *Clear the way!*

Women and children scramble out of burning buildings. A timber cracks under the weight of flames and falls to the street right in front of us.

"This way!" I shout, ducking into the nearest alley.

We are plunged into darkness. I grope for Kathleen's hand and she holds me with a grip to crush bones. She'd break my arm before she'd leave me behind. Sparks fly up like a fountain.

"Sweet Jesus, save us," Kathleen pants. Heat on top of the heat of the day blasts at us from all directions.

"Mother Mary, guide us," she gasps, as one way after another is heaped with flaming ruins.

We make detours. Run blocks out of our way, only to double back when that way is blocked, too.

"Angles and saints, defend us," she cries when the smoke is so thick we don't know which way to go.

And they do defend us, all the way to Mother Hildegard's door.

It's nearly dark when we squeeze through the bars of the locked gate and stand, gasping in the courtyard in front of the brick convent—a sanctuary in a city gone to ashes. Overhead thunder rolls and a great clap of lighting shows a crew of seven tall men standing before the convent door. One is the butcher, Ivan, who came to my aid when the officer tried to recruit me. He is in a blood-smeared butcher's apron with a cleaver in one hand and a grappling hook in the other. One is a soldier with a rifle on his shoulder. The rest are brewers of enormous girth and irregular weaponry.

"*Kinder raus!*" the oldest of the brewers shouts between claps of thunder. He waves us away from the doors.

"No!" Kathleen shouts. "We've come to see Mother Hildegard!"

"*Nein!*" another brewer says. "You will not pass."

The brewers stand shoulder to shoulder before the door, beefy arms crossed and soot-speckled faces scowling.

Kathleen looks from one to the next. "We aren't common brawlers. We've come to help her! Please."

I'm so weary I go to the statue of the Blessed Mother in the center of the courtyard and sit on the stone ledge where you're supposed to kneel. Mary and Joseph ran all the way to Egypt with Jesus. I'm sure she knows from tired.

"Dancing boy?" Ivan says, coming closer. I raise my hand, too weary even to speak.

Ivan sits beside me, his broad butcher's knife resting on his knee. "Mother and her sisters are gone from the house. Gone to do what's needed in this dark hour. We do not ask where they go. But she bid us to guard their door and the sanctity of this house with our last breath. Even against such lambs as you."

"There are flames and falling timbers out in the streets," Kathleen says, still on her feet and still scowling. "You—you! You enormous lump of bad sausage! I can't take my brother out in that. I won't!"

None of the men move.

"Mother Hildegard would not turn us away," she insists.

"Many are the needs this dark day," the oldest of the brewers says. "Many are the labors of Mother Hildegard and her sisters. Your needs are not the greatest among them."

"You Irish," says another, just as stern. "It's your own out there doing the lynching and the burning. What do you have to fear from your own?"

"You fat old men!" Kathleen shrieks. "What do you know of fear, you with your broad shoulders and your full plates! We have to fear what every woman fears her whole life long. Ye heartless men! When have you ever been small or hungry? Would you send a German child out on the streets this night? Aren't we Catholic like you? Don't we sit side by side in church?"

Ivan looks at the cobblestones of the courtyard and shuffles his feet. "It's not that we don't care, *Fräulein*. There's no room for you—"

The stoutest of the brewers clouts Ivan upside the head with a blow that would have buckled a man less sturdy than him.

"*Raus!*" he says to us, pointing to the street.

I give the butcher and the brewers a long look but their minds are made up. I reach for the only thing in the wide world that we own. Granny said it would save us someday and maybe it will. Maybe it works like some kind of relic from a holy well.

I kneel before the Blessed Mother and start to pray. Kathleen follows my lead and prays beside me. I could never fight these giants, but there is that bit in the Bible about faith moving mountains. I think about Daniel in his den of lions. He survived on a prayer. I close my eyes. Kathleen launches in on the litany of saints.

"Jesus, Mary, and Joseph," she says.

"Pray for us," I answer.

"St. Bridget."

"Pray for us."

I want to go to Big Al's theater so desperately. I want to find a place for us in the world. I give up *pretending* to be pious and pray like I have never prayed before. We have one sanctuary left and forty blocks of fire stand in the way.

"St. Christopher."

"Pray for us."

"St. Patrick—"

And at the name of my brother's patron saint, there is a roll of thunder so long and deep it rattles my teeth. Lightning splits the sky and rain pours down.

CHAPTER 21

I lift my face to the rain. Flashes of lightning flood the courtyard with light, only to plunge us back into darkness. Fat raindrops run down my cheeks, into my collar, and over my outstretched hands. Across the street the burning dry-goods shop sends up hisses of steam. The rain falls harder. Rioters outside the convent gate who were shouting and waving clubs moments before stop and turn their faces to the sky. We have needed rain in the city for weeks. Fire hydrants are down to a trickle of water. The guardians of the convent reach their arms out to the rain, smiling, clapping each other on the back. Out there in the burning streets are their own homes, their butcher shops and breweries. I turn to Kathleen and take the harp on my shoulders.

"I know you don't like the idea of the theater," I say. "Please, just this once. Trust me."

"It's all right," she says, holding an upturned palm to the rain. "I think I know a sign when I see one."

We head toward Union Park. The broken glass has an eerie sparkle from the yellow glow of dying fires and from every third or fourth gas lamp that isn't broken. Telegraph wires snake across the streets. Telegraph poles have been chopped down and laid across the trolley tracks. Four men stagger past with a mate on a stretcher made from a canvas awning. The wounded man drips blood and roars for his mother. A woman with a crowbar in hand stands watch over the body of a dead man draped in a coat. She is so drenched with rain, I can't tell if she's crying. A woman with three children in tow and a baby in arms settles them to sleep for the night in a doorway. She stands guard over them, spreading her skirt across their sleeping bodies.

"Rest, Ma," the oldest of them says. A boy almost as old as me. "Let me stand watch a while."

"Hush now," the mother says.

"There's nothing left for them to steal," he insists.

"It's wide awake I am."

She covers them over with her skirt and falls to humming a lullaby. Kathleen and I stand frozen across the street. That family was us, not six months ago. I still have my money from the dancing. I draw the rag with the coins knotted together out of my pocket, and the single silver dollar Big Al gave me, too.

"Can we spare it?"

"We cannot," Kathleen says. But she is rooted to the spot, too, lost in the memory of being evicted.

We should go. I want to go. There's a roof and shelter for us just a mile away. We've already seen a hundred tragedies today. They have floated past like phantoms in a dream. But this little family has me on a tether.

"Never," Kathleen whispers to herself, still mesmerized. "God help me, I will never be her."

There's always someone worse off than you, Da used to say. No matter how little was on our table, he'd take a bit of it to a neighbor in need. Or he'd give an evicted family passing through a place to bathe and clean their clothes. Ma used to purse her lips and fold her arms, like Kathleen is doing now. She'd scold him, to be sure, but she never stopped him.

I remember all too well the way people looked at us when we were sleeping in ditches and begging our way to the ships. The pity of folks who've got more than you, it sticks to you like tar. Long after you don't need their charity, you still feel the burn of it. I walk over to the woman in the doorway slowly, so she has plenty of time to size me up.

"I found this on the ground back there," I say, waving a hand toward no place in particular. "Maybe you dropped it?"

I hold out the pennies and nickels knotted together in a rag. She gives me a wary look.

"Anyone could have dropped it in the madness of the day," she says.

"Was the madness any fault of yours?"

"It was not!"

"Take it, then."

She holds out her hand and I drop the bundle of coins in. She opens her eyes a bit at the weight of it, but then closes her hand around it and brings it to her heart like you would a warm potato on a winter night.

"You're the jewel of your mother's house," she says to me, just like they used to say about Packy.

"Good evening to you, then," I say and back away.

We head down the Bowery, and doubt grabs hold and gives me a good shake. What if Big Al turns me down? What if he's gone away from town like all of the rest of the rich swells? It will be months before anyone's in the mood to toss a coin to a street corner dancer, no matter how good he is. And there won't be much call for lady's maids in the city either. I was a fool to give the money away.

The memory of hunger washes over me. There is a certain kind of ache when you wake up and it's still dark and you're still weary because you've been sleeping on stones. No matter how long I live, I will remember that weariness; it runs clean to the bone. I find Big Al's silver dollar in my pocket and wish on it like it's a fairy talisman.

From deep in the shadows I can smell the sour tang of spilled spirits and hear the drunken singing of "The Rising of the Moon." Kathleen nods in the direction of a looted bakery. There's nothing left in the place but crumbs and a great dusting of flour that has turned to paste in the rain.

"Don't fret now," she says. "There's nothing to buy."

It's true. With each block we pass, the cruel stupidity of the destruction sinks in. Things we need, bread and the bookshop, destroyed. The hardware store door hangs crooked on its hinges and the shelves are bare, but the brewery—untouched. One whole block torched and the next standing without a scratch. My heart sinks with each passing block. What if Big Al's theater is burned to the ground?

The church bell tolls the night prayer and puddles turn into sludgy streams and rats come up out of their flooded holes by the time we reach Canal Street.

The theater still stands, and Big Al is there in front with a torch in hand. To one side is a tattooed fellow with a long ferryman's hook and on the other the knife-thrower with a length of iron chain. The older man, Avrim the tailor, is in earnest conversation with a man in a butcher's apron. Big Al passes him a slip of paper and the fellow disappears into the dark.

"Big Al!" I shout.

His defenders swivel about to face me, and Big Al lifts his torch high.

"Daniel!" he shouts to me. "Avrim, do you see there? It's our Daniel, come home to us!"

I come up the steps, pulling Kathleen along behind me.

"What's kept you away all this time?"

"I was . . ." I turn to my sister. "Persuading my family to come."

Kathleen steps between me and the man with the chain. She surveys Big Al carefully. His usual fine topcoat and hat and silk tie are nowhere to be seen. His trousers are smudged with soot; his shirt rolled up to the elbows like a common day laborer.

"Kathleen," I say, giving her a pleading look. "This is Big Al."

"Alberto Fortino, at your service, Miss," he says.

"He doesn't look the part right now, but he's the owner of this grand theater. He offered me a job. A proper job with wages."

"Who are you to have business with my brother? A child!"

"He shows great promise as a showman, Miss Kathleen. A trained voice. Can dance a jig like a house on fire. An instinct for what the audience wants to hear, and something else besides. He's no spoiled society crooner. He sings and dances as if lives hang in the balance. Folk lean in to him. Like I've never seen before."

"Have you seen him on stage, Miss?" the man with the chain adds. "He's a headliner to be sure."

"But he's only a boy," Kathleen says.

I squirm in my shoes. I liked being fifteen.

"The younger, the better," Big Al says firmly.

"The audience loves a child act. They'll take him into their hearts, you'll see. They'll come back week after week and put down their hard-earned wages for that sweet voice and winning smile."

"A theater is not a fit life for a boy," Kathleen insists. "I won't have him among indecent people."

Big Al beams a smile at us both. "Miss Kathleen," he says, arm outstretched. "I see at once you're all the family this boy needs. A second Joan of Arc come to drive England," he gestures to the theater behind him, "out of France." He indicates me. "You'll run me a hard bargain, I can tell. This is all I ask of you. Stay with us for a day—just one day. If you find us unfit, I will trouble you no more."

Kathleen hesitates.

"My wife and daughter are within, ready to make you welcome," he says.

She hesitates some more.

"Brick walls," he adds. "Nothing to burn on the outside save the windowsills, and we've prepared for that." He points to a row of filled buckets on the top step. To the left is a scorched windowsill. But not a single pane of glass is broken. "We will stand guard upon this door all night and all day tomorrow and all week if we have to."

"The riots are done," I say, waving to the nearly empty street behind me. "The rain stopped it," I add proudly, since my prayers at the convent earlier were my contribution to the events of the day.

"Not likely," says the man with the chain.

"Can't you hear them?" says the ferryman. He points across the street with his hook. From deep in a basement I can hear off-key singing. 'Rory O'Moore' is the hero on their lips, and it'll be 'Father Murphy from County Wexford' next, no doubt. Rebels all.

Avrim motions us to come inside. "The brewer lost a valiant battle this evening. The mob overran his shop and made off with every keg of stout he had on the premises." Avrim takes off his spectacles and wipes away the grime. "They'll drink themselves to sleep in alleyways all over town tonight. And when they wake up there will be nothing but half-brewed beer for breakfast."

"You can imagine how well that will go over come sunrise when it's hot again, and humid and muddy," Big Al says.

"This could go on for another day?" Kathleen says.

"At least one more day," Big Al says.

"Maybe more," Avrim adds with a shrug and

upturned hands. "So much anger. And who will stop them? There are not enough policemen in New York to do it."

"You'll be safe here," Big Al says soothingly. "No one will come through these doors to harm you. I give you my word."

"I accept your terms, Mr. Fortino," Kathleen says. "At least for one day."

Big Al puts a hand to his heart and gives her a small bow.

"We have an accord," he says. "Come meet my family."

I'm nervous all over again for Kathleen to meet Mrs. Fortino. She is sitting at the kitchen table with little Angelo in her arms. She has her spare hand on the shoulder of one of the little boys.

"Angel of God, my guardian dear," the boy says, head bowed and little hands clasped firmly together in a great exertion of prayer. Kathleen sighs to see it.

We wait by the door while the one twin and then the other says his bedtime prayer and gets his blessing. Kathleen takes in the tidy hearth, the two older boys wiping dishes, the cross over the mantle and the row of books—books!—on the windowsill. I shouldn't have worried.

The twins scurry to their trundle beds beside the hearth and Mrs. Fortino spies us by the door.

"Thank heaven you've found your way," she says, coming over. She cups my face with her hand. "I've worried about you all the long day! And this must be your sister."

"Mrs. Fortino," I say, remembering how proper introductions went at the Treadwell house. "May I present Miss Kathleen O'Carolan."

Kathleen gives a small curtsey and says, "Ma'am."

"A grown sister," Mrs. Fortino says approvingly. "And handsome besides. Come, my dears, you mustn't stand another minute. I can see by the look of you, you've been on your feet all day. Eat!"

Suddenly the one potato we shared for lunch feels like three days ago. In a shot she's got us settled on a bench with cheese and bread before us. I shovel it in but Kathleen hesitates. At the Treadwell's we never ate where the lady of the house could see us.

"Come now," Mrs Fortino says gently. "Your brother will be a member of our theater family, but you, my dear—I hope that you will consent to be my companion. A woman always treasures another woman in the house. Will you?"

"Yes, ma'am," Kathleen says. "I'd like that."

A girl with curly black hair comes into the room, the piccolo player from my audition. She has a doll in one arm and a book under the other.

"And here's someone else who will be glad for another woman in the house. Bianca! Look who's come. It's Daniel's sister."

"A sister?" Bianca says, breaking into a broad smile and showing the one missing tooth. "At last! Will you read to me?"

"Honestly, Bianca, Miss Kathleen has been out in this mayhem all day. She's exhausted."

"I don't mind," Kathleen says. "I like to read." She makes a space on the bench for Bianca to slide in.

"*The Swiss Family Robinson*, by Johann Wyss," she begins. She slides the candle a bit closer and points to the words as she's reading so her pupil can follow along.

> "*For many days we had been tempest-tossed. Six times had the darkness closed over a wild and terrific scene, and returning light had often brought but renewed distress, for the raging storm had increased in fury until on the seventh day all hope was lost . . .*"

She reads with good spirit, tired as she is, and Bianca leans in, captured by the story like I get captured by a song. I try to pay attention, but once my belly is full I feel the room swim before my eyes and put my head on the table just to hold things still.

★★★

I wake up hours later stretched out on the kitchen bench. The sounds of the riot are raging again outside the sanctuary of Mrs. Fortino's kitchen. It's already a sweltering day. The older boys are nowhere to be seen and Gustav the knife thrower is fast asleep in the rocking chair by the window. Big Al and Mrs. Fortino and Avrim the tailor are in a hushed conversation around the kitchen sink.

"Don't fret, Margaret," Big Al says. "It's only firefighters and looters abroad now. The boys will be fine; they're just outside the door."

"The fire buckets are spent," Mrs. Fortino says. "And look." She turns the watercock and the barest trickle comes out. "All these fires, they've dropped the reservoir."

"You are wise to keep the rain barrels," Avrim says.

"You'll not touch the rain barrels," Mrs. Fortino says fiercely. "What will we drink? What will I use to wash the wounds you are so set on getting?" She waves an accusing finger at the streak of blood that goes down the side of Big Al's face. Avrim has a bandage wrapped around his left hand.

She leans in closer to whisper, "If anyone were to find out, we'd be dragged into the street and stoned. And the children too. There's no mercy in that mob."

Any thought I had of sitting up and making myself known flies away. I freeze in place, closing my eyes and forcing the long slow breaths of sleep in spite of my rising panic.

"Margaret, my life, my light, I swear before the angels, no one was left to see us take them in."

"It was a feat of theatrical fire," Avrim says. "I have never seen the like. And neither had the rabble. It ran them off, every last one."

"All blessings on the union of saltpeter, brimstone, and gunpowder," Big Al adds with a boyish grin. "I have missed my magic shows. And I had a little store of flash-bang left over from the passion play at Easter."

"You are the devil's own!" Mrs. Fortino says with

just a hint of pride in her voice, but I hear a grunt from Big Al which I know from sore experience is the sound of a man who's had his ear tweaked.

"Blame me, good lady," Avrim says gently. "For I could not bear to see even a dog beaten as these men were."

"Before my own door," Big Al says. "What could I do?"

"And you're sure no one saw?" Mrs. Fortino presses.

"Took them in through the cellar. Hid them under the stage. There's only the trapdoor and we piled all the sandbags from the stage rigging before the cellar door. None could break in there, not even with torches."

"Will they live, do you think?"

"They will," says Avrim firmly. "There's many hurt worse, sheltering in the basement of the police station. And all those orphans from the asylum, too."

My heart races, remembering my own run through the fires to get here. I don't know how you'd ever do it with a string of a hundred orphans in tow.

"It's only for a day," Big Al says, "while the mob cools off."

"What if this riot lasts two days or three?" Mrs. Fortino says. "What if it lasts a week?"

"Unheard of," Big Al says.

"This entire riot is unheard of. Our friends! Our neighbors! One man sets fire to a building and his son is on the fire engine risking his life to put it out. Women abroad in the streets with knives, doing unspeakable things. It's madness and no knowing when it will end. Get rest, the both of you, for I fear worse is to come."

Mrs. Fortino busies herself in the kitchen. I stick to my spot on the bench, washed over with memories of home. Why did we come? Everyone said it would be better in America, but it's the same thing all over again. Rich swells lording it over the poor. Folk beaten for being what they are. Wars fought and men pressed into service, only to die among strangers. Isn't there anywhere a body can go and really be free?

I fret over it until the twins wake up and crowd onto the bench clamoring for their porridge. I sit up and strive not to think on all I've heard

***

In the days that follow I can think of nothing else. In sweltering heat we board up broken windows and in pouring rain we shore up barricades around the doors. We keep watch from the rooftop and from there I see the worst that one human can do to another.

But as the second day of terror draws to a close I see other things. The courage of policemen is the greatest shock—and in defense of the common man, too. When the mob gathers ready to put a tenement to the torch and bludgeon the folk when they come running out, the coppers come down the street, six abreast, beating the ground with their nightsticks as they come. The firemen and their pumpers close behind. They beat their way through until the will of the mob wavers. As the mob scatters the coppers call out to them, appealing to their pride and patriotism. Shouting for them to go home to their families and protect them they love.

There are quieter surprises. The doctor who comes to call at all hours of the night, with no protection but a torch to light his way and the black leather satchel such men of healing carry. The longshoremen, most brutal of the fighters, even they take boats in cover of darkness to bring bread across the east river—baskets of bread passed from house to house. The women take in an orphaned babe. They pass her secretly from woman to woman. Each one nurses the babe in turn.

"For love of her mother," says Mrs. Fortino when the babe comes to her door.

She is as golden brown as a little hazelnut and with hazel eyes, too. I've heard tell of the fate that befalls women at the hands of the mob who marry a man not their own race—as brutal and cruel a fate as any man's. And women are right in the thick of it, doing violence and suffering it in equal share.

"What will become of her?" Kathleen whispers, rocking Angelo while Mrs. Fortino feeds the babe.

"Her father's at sea. Serves on a navy ship. He was as true-hearted a man as anyone would wish for their daughter to marry. Katie was happy with him. We mothers must shelter their child until he comes home."

"Black men serve in the navy?" Kathleen says. "I've read nothing about it!"

Mrs. Fortino nods. "There's hardly a ship in the world without black crew members aboard."

For each man who hurls a brick through our windows or threatens us with fire, another stops by in the quiet moments to see that we're safe and offer the kind of swagger that passes for encouragement among men.

"We've seen worse at the hands of the English, haven't we!" says one, as he shares out a measure of flour he's bought at the only bakery in miles that isn't burned down.

"We'll weather this storm. See if we don't," says another as he takes a can of beans and a bit of lamp oil from Big Al.

"You should have seen the other fella," says a neighbor so wreathed around in bandages you could scarce see his face.

I come to love my fellow hard-headed, tough-minded New Yorkers, who are still tender at the middle like a good loaf of bread.

★★★

Three weary days later, we hear drums from the rooftop and the steady tromping feet of the Union army. They wear blue coats and trousers, stiff with mud and stained with the blood and powder scorches of battle. Straight from Gettysburg, they have come without rest. Thousands died at Gettysburg.

Thousands. And yet here are a thousand more. They march in rows, our own Irish Brigade among them.

The mob sees their friends and neighbors in uniform and cheers. "Come join us!" they cry out. "All of us together, we can't fail."

Not a single soldier breaks ranks. Behind them come the artillery. Horses and mules pull the long guns into place. Officers on horseback call orders. The drummers change cadence to signal the marching men. It's a thing to behold after days of chaos, a unit of men moving in step together, facing down danger as one.

They don't flinch. They don't look away, not for a moment. It's grim faced the soldiers are, they've marched past their own homes in flames, seen their own neighbors behaving like wild creatures, and them with a war to win.

They march right to the center of their own neighborhood. They take a position. The drums fall silent. Upon a single shout of command, they load their cannons. Aim their rifles and fire.

The mob goes down, like summer hay before the mowers. When the smoke clears, men and women alike, even children, have been shot dead there on the cobblestones before their own homes.

The remains of the mob don't scatter this time. They surrender. Arms in the air, weeping over their lost. Hiding their faces for shame. Looking on their neighborhood now, not with the eyes of anger, but with horror at what their actions let loose. The mob only wanted to stay out of the war, and all they did was bring it right to our front door.

THE RIOT SUBSIDING: A LAST
DESPERATE STRUGGLE.
TRIUMPH OF THE MILITARY.
SEVERAL RINGLEADERS CAUGHT.

—*New York Times*

CHAPTER 22

FRIDAY, JULY 17, 1863

At dawn on Friday, I wake up in my blanket roll in the boys' bedroom. Mrs. Fortino is asleep in the kitchen rocking chair with baby Angelo. I climb up to the rooftop to take my turn from Paolo at standing watch. The fires have all gone out, but ashes carried on the wind give the air a certain shimmer.

"Any news?"

"Quiet all night," Paolo says.

"Any eggs yet?"

Mrs. Fortino is a magician in the kitchen. She mixes up flour and eggs and rolls it thin as a whisker. Then she cuts long strips and boils the whole thing instead of baking. Pasta, they call it. Best food on earth. We all sit around the same table like family. She keeps a little garden up on the roof with rows of bean and tomato plants and in the corner a chicken coop.

"No eggs yet," Paolo says to me. "The smoke throws them off laying. Sing to them. Chickens like that." And then he heads wearily down the ladder to sleep.

I like Big Al's sons. They are nothing like my own brothers. They've never been hungry, or slept out on the road. They know games I've never played—checkers and cards. But they don't laugh or lord it over me. Even better, they each have a musical instrument of their own to play. I've always wanted my own instrument. Sometimes when there's a spare minute, I take out the sheet of music I stole from the Treadwell house and try to pick out "Beautiful Dreamer" on the piano.

The morning is clear and I stand on the roof of the theater like a king in his tower. I look down the long avenues and see soldiers at every intersection, rifles on their shoulders. The harbor pilots are guiding ships into their docks to unload. Longshoremen, many with bandages wound around their heads, walk to the docks. Women head for the factories. Street sweepers begin the weary work of cleaning up.

I see a long lumber wagon heading toward me. It is driven by a nun in a flowing black habit.

I take the stairs at a run. Big Al and Avrim are at the table with Baby Angelo and the twins.

"Kathleen!" I shout. "I think it's Mother Hildegard coming down the street. Driving a wagon and all."

"Driving a wagon?" she says.

"A lumber wagon. It's huge."

Big Al laughs. "That'll be Mother Hildegard for certain," he says. "A finger in every pie, that woman, and lucky we are for it. Margaret, have our guests make ready to leave."

A shiver of doubt runs up my neck. Did he change his mind about hiring me? We haven't talked about the show or my contract since I set foot inside the theater; we've been so busy defending it. Did he send for Mother Hildegard to take us to Blackwell's Island after all? I glance at Kathleen.

"No one is taking you anywhere," she whispers.

She edges us toward the cabinet where she has stashed the harp. She takes it out and holds it behind her back, ready to make a run for it.

Big Al goes to the stage. He lifts up a trap door. Two black men come out blinking in the light of day. It's Samuel and Isaac. And now I get a shiver of plain fear. They're covered in bruises, eyes swollen, clothes tattered, and walking like old men.

I knew someone was there. Knew what Big Al and Avrim risked to rescue them. Knew that Mrs. Fortino was slipping them food when nobody was looking. But I didn't think until now that they'd be someone I know. I didn't think about what they suffered before they made it to our door or what they lost while they were hiding or how they will live now that it's over. Before I can think what to say, Mother Hildegard comes in with Mrs. Fortino.

"Kathleen," she says. "Thank heavens you're safe. And who is this?" she adds, turning to me.

"Daniel is one of us now," Mrs. Fortino says. "Our new song and dance man." She looks at Big Al a little nervously. "Or at least we hope so."

"Is he now?" Mother Hildegard says. "And can you be wholly yourself here?" she adds lightly.

It's only been five days and I already forget what it was like to go about in a dress and be a meek housemaid. Last night I sat on the floor—on the floor!—and played marbles with Vincent and Anthony for an hour. They give me a boy's chores. I don't have to guard what I do and say every moment.

"I can," I say with a lump in my throat. There is so much more to say than that; I didn't know how much I missed being a boy among brothers.

"I heard you came by the convent while I was away," Mother Hildegard says.

"We did," Kathleen says. "When our employer stole our money and abandoned us, our first thought was to come to you."

"And my faithful brewers and butchers turned you away," Mother Hildegard says, voice full of concern. We both nod.

"I am sorry. We were packed to the rafters with other guests. Safer for everybody if you didn't know."

"Good trouble," Kathleen says with a smile. "I understand."

Mother Hildegard beams at her. "I thought you might. As I said before, you have the look of a great resister."

She turns away from us and I'm the only one who sees Kathleen flushed with pride.

"Alberto," Mother Hildegard says, "I received a very mysterious and poorly spelled message from you about the urgent delivery of two packages." She gives a meaningful nod in the direction of the carpenters. "It took me a few days and some intemperate bargaining to secure a wagon and horses. And we've had many other deliveries to make. But here I am. How may I serve you?"

Big Al is all smiles. "Mother Hildegard, are you still distilling the most excellent brandy in all of New York in your cellar?"

"I'm sure I don't know what you're talking about. I am a resourceful woman. That's all that need be said."

Everyone laughs, even the little boys.

"Mother," Big Al says. "Here are Samuel and Isaac, as fine a pair of carpenters as you'll find in the city. Fellas," he says, turning to Samuel and Isaac. "Mother Hildegard is as canny as a prince and as wise as the pope. I would trust her with my life."

"I have a lumber wagon with plenty of room to hide you. I'll take you out of the city, if that is your wish."

Isaac and Samuel exchange a wary glance. I can't even imagine what it was like to be hidden away, hearing the riot, but not able to see any of it—just waiting there in the dark for the worst to happen. I've seen my share of trouble, but nothing like this.

"I have brothers in the city, ma'am," Isaac says. "For all your kindness I could not abandon them. Let me search for them and we will go together."

"Black families have fled the city," Mother Hildegard says. "Many are now sheltering in Brooklyn. Others in New Jersey. Surely your people will be among them."

"How do we know you'll bring us to safety? After all that's happened, why should we trust you?" Samuel says. His face is so swollen I can't read his expression.

Mother Hildegard sighs. "Why indeed. We none of us have cause to trust each other. On this journey we will pass through many a lonely stretch of road. My sisters and I are women, unarmed, and unaccustomed to fighting. And you have every just reason to hate us. You might harm us. You might steal the wagon. Yet I will trust you. Not because I know you to be an honest man but because I find hope in choosing to trust. And hope in this dark hour is what I desire more than safety."

I take a look at the stout brick walls around me. All I've thought of since I set foot ashore was finding a place like this—a place of safety, somewhere we can live without dying. I've thought little of the safety of others. But in the worst of the trouble, Big Al risked his life and the lives of his family—on a magic trick—an illusion of fire and cannon fire. All to save the lives of carpenters who are no kin to him. Kathleen would murder me outright if I ever did such a dangerous thing. But I confess, right now, I like the idea of it.

"The sisters are seldom challenged as they go about their work," Mrs. Fortino says. "Surely they will bring you to safety."

"And no doubt you have a bottle or two of your excellent brandy to smooth the way." Big Al says, winking at Mother Hildegard. "Nothing lubricates free passage so well."

"I will carry you across the water to New Jersey if that is what you wish. But my wagon carries medicine and bandages and soap," Mother Hildegard says. "The field hospital outside of Gettysburg is in grave need. We will not be stopped or searched on a mission of mercy. I will take you all the way to Gettysburg if you wish. You will find many of your fellow New Yorkers when you arrive."

"Thank you, ma'am," Isaac says with his cap in

hand. "Is it true the army is taking colored regiments at last? I'll work in the hospital if I must, but I've got family down South and I'm ready to fight for them. Long ready. I was ready from the beginning."

"The colored regiments are forming farther north," Kathleen says. "Massachusetts, say the papers. It's a fearful long way from here."

"I'll walk," Isaac says. "Clear to Maine if I have to."

"The Union army?" Samuel says. "We'll just trade one cage for another. What difference between an officer and a master when both can command you to throw your life away?"

"There is little safety for any of us in this life," Mother says, looking particularly at Avrim, who nods in sad agreement. "But if you are of a mind to leave this country, I can recommend you to a convent in Toronto. They are building a hospital there and have much need of skilled carpenters."

"Black troops will see combat and soon," Big Al says. "When people see you fighting shoulder to shoulder with the rest of the army, they'll see your quality."

"Speaking of quality," Mother Hildegard says, "what is this I see?" She gestures to a wooden box with a slot in the top.

"We had all that time down there under the trap door," Samuel says. "Nothing to do, but plenty of scraps of lumber around."

"Big Al said you'd help us, so we built you a poor box by way of a thank you."

I slide in beside the men to admire their work. "May we keep it here, Mother?" I say. "We could post it right by the front door."

"A poor box in a theater? Unheard of!" Mother says.

"Music has a way of making a man more kindly disposed to his fellow creatures," I say, remembering the folk who stood between me and the recruiter when I was singing for pennies. "You might be surprised."

If I have any say in it, I want to use the money from the poor box to buy tools for them that lost their work in the fires. A man should have the tools of his trade.

"I'll need help from every corner," Mother Hildegard says. "We lost the roof of the school to cannon fire yesterday."

"Cannon fire?! Who would shoot at a school?" Kathleen bursts out.

"I admit it hurt me to the heart when I saw those flames," Mother says "But sometimes good comes out of bad. The bishop has given his blessing to build a school three times bigger." She gives Kathleen a meaningful nod. "Where will I ever find enough teachers for a school so large?"

A look passes between the two of them. I put my arm around Kathleen. She is the plague of my life, but I won't have her gone from me entirely. Mother has plenty of other sisters. I've only got one.

Mother Hildegard smiles at me. "A woman must be seventeen to sit for a teacher's exam and eighteen to teach in a classroom," she says.

"I'm teaching now!" Kathleen says, gesturing to the table strewn with newspapers and pencils.

"She does have a knack for it," Mrs. Fortino says. "And thank goodness. I've got more than I can do keeping this household fed. The schoolwork always fell by." She comes and takes Kathleen's hand. "Already we'd miss you if you leave us for the convent. Not that I'd ever speak a word against holy orders."

"You have time yet," Mother Hildegard says. "I'll be coming for the poor box every month. We'll speak more on this in time."

"The ferry leaves in thirty minutes," Avrim says, pocket watch in hand.

Mrs. Fortino wraps up bread in a cloth. She hands it to Isaac and a small paper package of salt to Samuel. They have nothing else to carry with them. I wish I had something to give besides hope that things will get better.

"Wait," Big Al says. "Here's your week's wages." He presses coins into their hands. "Don't you leave New York forever. Sounds to me like Mother Hildegard is going to need carpenters, and plenty of them."

Mother Hildegard sweeps out the door and the carpenters after her. Everyone else watches them go, so they don't see the look that passes between Big Al and his wife. I've seen that look before and nothing good ever followed it.

CHAPTER 23

"Bianca," Mrs. Fortino says after they go. "Take the boys to play up onstage for a bit."

Anthony and Vincent run off calling dibs on the ball and the juggling rings. Kathleen tucks the harp back in the cupboard and follows them.

"The money's all gone, isn't it?" I say when the room is quiet.

"What? No!" says Big Al.

"What on earth gave you that idea?" says Mrs. Fortino.

Avrim gives me a shrewd look and closes his watch. It was once a fine piece, but it's dented, and the hinge is held together with wire.

"The boy has eyes to see," Avrim says. "And

though he and his sister have shown uncommon courage in the last five days, this riot is not the greatest hardship they have endured—if I am any judge of hearts at all."

Avrim is usually so quiet. Always mending something. I hardly notice him.

"It's not easy to be Catholic in Ireland, is it?" he says.

I shake my head.

"It is not easy to be a Jew anywhere. And like me, you have lost your family, save for this one sister."

I nod.

"You should know this. The Fortino family is among the most generous I have known these last five years. But in his great care for his theater family, Mr. Fortino puts a good face on trouble when the truth would serve him better."

"Now Avrim, there's no need to worry the child," Big Al begins, but Avrim cuts him off.

"He is not *your* child. And if you cannot give the contract you promised, you must tell them, so they can decide—will they cast their lot in with you, or no?"

I gasp like I've been struck in the chest. I thought I had finally found a place—a home. "What does he mean? Aren't you going to fix the theater?"

Kathleen steps up behind me, arm around my shoulder. We face them side by side, like always, just us two.

"No," Big Al says with a heavy sigh. "Not today." He presses his hands flat on the table. "But I will fix it. Soon. I believe in variety theater and clean family entertainment. We can bring people more than liquid joy. I know we can!"

"I can't see how," Mrs. Fortino says. "We've taken all the savings we had to build the theater and now we have to replace every window."

"I've worked the docks before," Big Al says. "I'll work them again. Alberto Jr. is old enough to put in a man's day. Paolo's a good worker, too."

"Paolo is thirteen!" Mrs. Fortino says. "He's still a boy! I won't have it."

"Not the docks for him, of course not." Big Al says. "But you know his character. He'll want to help."

Mrs. Fortino does that thing that apparently all women do with the folding of the arms and the tapping of the foot.

"We will find a way," Big Al says. "We always have."

"I also observe," Avrim goes on, "that the newest

members of our theater family have not been entirely honest either."

Kathleen gives him a stare, arms likewise folded across her chest, lips pursed, and foot a-tapping.

"They brought with them a bundle which they have not opened since they arrived, so it must contain neither food nor clothing. They have hidden it from sight, but the sister checks on it through the day as though she fears it will be taken from her. Perhaps it is a token of memory from home, nothing more. But they came to us after a day when hundreds of wealthy homes were looted. She worked as a maid. Perhaps this thing is stolen."

Kathleen gets pink in the face.

"I do not condemn you," he goes on in a mild voice. He's a braver man than he looks, to keep speaking when Kathleen is mere moments from taking a rolling pin to his tender parts.

"I know the temptation of hunger and the fear of living in the street. But mark my words." He turns to Big Al. "Police will come searching in this neighborhood for the stolen property of the wealthy. And if they find it here, we may not be able to prevent them from taking both these children to Blackwell's Island. I would not condemn the meanest dog to live in such a place. If this is true—let us help you, before you are in trouble beyond our help."

"We're not thieves," I say hotly.

"It's ours and our ancestors' before us," Kathleen says, just as mad.

"A family heirloom then?" Avrim says.

"It's our treasure," Kathleen says. "Granny said it's always saved us in the past. She said it will save us again in our hour of greatest need."

"How?" I turn to Kathleen, suddenly angry at her though I'm not sure why. "It's a broken harp that neither of us can play."

"She made me swear to guard it."

"What does it matter now? It's not a crime to own a harp in America. It's not worth anything. Why are you still carrying it?"

Kathleen hangs her head. "I can't let it go."

"May I see it?" Avrim says quietly. "I won't take it. I give you my word."

Kathleen hesitates.

"*Whensoever the evil spirit from the Lord was upon Saul,*" Avrim quotes, "*David took his harp, and played with his hand, and Saul was refreshed, and was better, for the evil spirit departed from him.*" Avrim gives a great sigh. "The harp is precious to my people also."

I go to the cabinet and unwrap the harp. It looks even more awful than I remembered. I feel a stab of shame. It's greenish-black and dusty, none of the glossy polish of a piano. The gut strings have split and peeled. Compared to Paolo's cello it looks like a piece of garbage. Nevertheless, Avrim cradles it with great care. He brings it into the light from the window.

"Such a shape as this—the curve of the neck and the strings so close together—modern harp-makers do not fashion them so."

"How is a tailor such an authority on music?" Kathleen says warily.

"I have been many things in my lifetime," Avrim says. "A clockmaker. A music teacher. A prisoner. A day laborer." He looks at her with the deepest sorrow. "A husband. A father."

Kathleen flushes pink all over again and looks at the floor. "I'm sorry," she says. "I used to think nobody in the whole world has suffered like the Irish." She looks toward the trap door where Samuel and Isaac had been hiding. "Now I just wish it were true."

Avrim smiles at her. "Through all my sorrows I have been a lover of music. It's a rare gift in a weary world."

He runs his fingers along the pillar and neck of the harp. "See here—something is scratched into the neck. And just where there is a missing string. It's quite faint."

He tilts the harp toward the light.

"1798. Does that date mean anything to you?"

My heart beats faster. I know songs about the terrors of the rebellion of 1798. I come closer. Trace my finger along the neck to the next missing string.

"1845," I read and then find the next missing string. "This one says 1847."

"*An Górta Mór*," Kathleen whispers. "The Great Hunger."

"Daniel, will you sound this string," Avrim says gently. "This one right here in the middle."

I give it a pluck and it makes a flat buzz.

"A gut string becomes brittle and breaks after a few decades, even in a harp as carefully tended as this. I think there is something underneath this, may I look?"

"It's already broken," I say.

Avrim carefully peels bits and pieces of the dried gut away. I see a glimmer of brightness. He strips away the whole thing and holds the harp up to the window again. Underneath the covering is a harp string of pure gold.

"Now try." He holds the harp out to me and I pluck the string. It rings out clear and bright, with an unearthly lightness in tone. It's a sound to call fairies out of their mountain halls and wake the souls of trees.

Kathleen searches the neck where the biggest string is missing. We lean in together to look for a date.

"1856," she says.

I get another chill up my spine. I was five years old when Da was transported to Australia for stealing.

"I remember," Kathleen says. "I was nine. The landlord raised the rent to clear us and all our neighbors off the land. Da wasn't having it. He went off one day and came back with money, more money than any of us had ever seen. Rent enough for us and all our neighbors, and sacks of flour and butter and cheese besides. The landlord had him clapped in irons by sundown. The next day he was sentenced to transportation."

"For selling his own property?" Mr. Fortino looks from me to Kathleen. "How can this be?"

"Can't testify in court if you're Catholic," I say. "And it's against the law to own a harp, too."

I take the harp from Avrim and give the sound-board a closer look. A bit of the greenish-black covering flakes off. I pick at it and a whole chip of it comes off. It's thicker and softer than paint.

"What is this?" I hold the flake out to Avrim.

He rolls it between his fingers. "How long has your family had this harp?"

I try to remember how far back the story goes.

"Six generations? Maybe? Or seven."

I scratch off a few more chips and put them in a saucer for a better look by the light of the window. The saucer is still warm. The chips go soft and round on the edges.

"Avrim," I say, showing him the saucer. "Where's your iron?"

He points to the stove and then gets a clean scrap from his ragbag.

"Use this," he says.

I take the rag and press it between the iron and stovetop until it's almost too hot to handle. And then I press it to the pillar of the harp and rub very gently in a small circle. The greenish-black covering melts and seeps into the cloth as I rub.

"Beeswax," Avrim says. "Astonishing."

He brings me a fistful of fresh rags. He begins

heating them up for me. As one cloth fills up with melted wax he hands me another. The wood underneath is dark at first but then lightens to a honey brown with swirls and spirals of gold and gleaming white stones. When we have cleared away a patch the size of my hand, I hold it up to the light. Big Al gasps in amazement and Kathleen puts a trembling hand on my shoulder. There is a pattern in gold of twining vines and glowing white berries. I've never seen the like of it. So intricate, no human could have made it. No wonder Granny believed in the fairies.

"Such a treasure," Avrim says, almost reverently. "This is very old. These inlays are gold and pearl. Do you know anything about where it came from?"

"Granny was dying when she told me about it," Kathleen says. "It was a gift from a prince. She must have known about the gold strings, but I don't think she knew what was under the wax."

This changes everything. We could sell the harp, not just a string at a time. We could sell the whole thing. We'd be rich. We'd be safe. I can see Kathleen putting together the same thought. All the weight of taking care of us could be lifted from her in one stroke.

"All this time," she says in a whisper. "We've been carrying it all this time. Anyone could have taken it from us. We could have lost it, not knowing."

The vision of just us two in a house of our own with a mountain of food flashes through my head. And at the same time, I'm dying to hear what the harp sounds like when all the strings are uncovered and the sounding board polished. I pluck the golden string again trying to place the note in a familiar song. I set the harp on the table and lean the sound-board against my heart. I reach down for the low strings with my right hand and the high strings with my left. I remember what the maestro taught me about chords.

"Look at you," Kathleen says softly. "A harper out of legend."

She runs her finger over the gold and pearl inlay. "Maybe we don't have to sell the whole thing. Maybe just one more string. To buy us time while I get a proper job and a place of our own." She looks to Avrim. "Or maybe two. How much is gold worth?"

"In wartime? Gold is worth a lot," Avrim says.

I look around the room. It's a shamble, to be honest. Breakfast still on the table, stack of dishes by the sink, toy blocks in a corner, and sheet music everywhere.

"I don't want a place of our own," I say. "I want to stay here. I want to sing and dance for my daily bread, here with people who want us. Who cares about being rich as long as we aren't starving? Have you met a rich person so far that you've liked?"

Kathleen puts a hand on my shoulder, gently for once.

"Are you sure?"

"I am. Let's sell a string, maybe two, so that we can open this theater and give some joy to people, ordinary people. Doesn't that sound better than being rich all on our own?"

"Two medium strings or one large would probably be enough," Avrim says. "Three months for the work, maybe four, and you could have your grand opening."

"In time for Christmas," Mrs. Fortino says.

Big Al looks at us in amazement. "After the hardest week in our lives, you would still cast your lot in with ours?"

Kathleen lifts up her chin and squares her shoulders to the man. "This has not been the hardest week of my life. Not even close. But why speak of casting lots? We should speak of contracts. If Daniel and I share our treasure with you, then we will need a share in the ownership of the theater."

Avrim laughs and claps his hands together. "A scholar!" he says, "Oh, she's a sharp one."

"I knew you'd drive me a hard bargain," Big Al says. "Knew it from the start. Didn't I say so?"

Mrs. Fortino takes Kathleen's hands in hers. "Do you know what you're signing on for?" she says. "If we form a partnership you'll gain when we gain, but you'll lose if we lose."

"I know," she says. "But what else will I do with him? There's no getting the dance out of the boy. I've tried."

Big Al whoops for joy. He scoops up his wife in a hug and lifts her from the ground.

"Oh, my friends," he says. "Can you imagine it? Every family out there has at least one heartstring tied to a soldier who fought under the green flag with the golden harp. Do you think they won't come to hear you? Daniel, you will break their hearts and knit them back together with this harp."

I squirm a little in my shoes, not quite daring to hope. "You mean the harp with missing strings that I don't know how to play?"

"A harp can be mended. And as for playing it—you'll learn. You'll play it as no one has for a hundred years."

I take the harp in my arms and lean the soundboard against my heart. I run my fingers over the remaining strings still covered in their gut string wrappers until I come to the one shining string we uncovered. I run my finger up and down its length, so smooth after hundreds of years buried. Still bright after centuries of darkness. I pluck it, and the same bell tone fills the room, but this time I feel it deep in my chest. The whole harp vibrates like a living thing—a thing that I have made to live with my own hands.

THE HEROES OF JULY: A Solemn and Imposing Event. Dedication of the National Cemetery at Gettysburg.

—*New York Times*

CHAPTER 24

FRIDAY, NOVEMBER 20, 1863

"*Four score and seven years ago . . .*"

Little Anthony sits beside Kathleen at the kitchen table and reads aloud, following her finger along in the newspaper.

". . . *our forefathers brought forth on this . . . con-tin-ent . . .*" He pauses to look to Kathleen for a nod of approval. "*A new nation . . .*"

"Conceived," Kathleen fills in.

". . . *In liberty and . . .*"

"Dedicated to the proposition," Kathleen fills in again. Vincent leans in, eager as always, to show up his twin brother.

"That all men are created equal!" he shouts.

"Now we are engaged in a great civil war, testing whether that nation, or any nation . . ." Vincent goes on.

"So conceived and so dedicated," Kathleen says.

"Can long endure," Anthony finishes.

Kathleen covers the page with her hand. "Endure. Bianca?"

"E-N-D-U-R-E. Endure," Bianca says. "To undergo hardship without giving in."

"Yes!" Kathleen says. "Daniel?"

"Endure," I say from across the table where I am finishing up mathematics problems on a slate. "We have endured four months of repairs and rehearsals and now it's opening night!"

"Now follow along. I'm going to read out the rest of Mr. Lincoln's speech," Kathleen says to Anthony and Vincent.

"We are met on a great battlefield of that war. We have come to dedicate a portion of that field . . ."

As she reads, Mrs. Fortino stops stirring the pasta sauce and listens. Gustav, the knife thrower, goes past in the hall and stops at the door to listen. Paolo stops tuning his cello and Bianca stops fussing Alberto Jr. about his costume. I set the slate aside, pull on my new dance shoes, and start warming up.

"It is for us the living, rather, to be dedicated here to the unfinished work which they who fought here have thus far so nobly advanced . . ."

That Lincoln, he can really turn a phrase. Somebody should put his speeches to music.

Gustav gestures to me to stop jumping and listen. My mind is wrapped up in the show that will start in an hour.

". . . that we here highly resolve that these dead shall not have died in vain . . ."

I know that Lincoln means the soldiers who died at Gettysburg. I know he means the great work of ending the civil war and building up all the things that the war has broken.

But I can't think of that, not today. Ever since sunup I have been thinking of my family. They dedicated themselves to getting me here, alive. And now I finally have a way to say—out loud in a theater full of people—that they didn't die in vain. Kathleen has her heart set on the convent, and everyone can see she's got the inner starch to take Mother Hildegard's place someday. For me, singing and dancing is enough. If I have to be the last of the name, I'm going to make it a name to remember.

Big Al comes in the kitchen with the rest of the cast. Mrs. Fortino sets bread and salt on the table and we stand in a circle around it. He has a word of thanks for everyone and then a moment of silence so we can all pray in our own languages—although, to be honest, I think Gustav might be striking a bargain with the god of knives and luck in German. He doesn't really seem like the praying type. Big Al turns to me when we are done.

"Thirty minutes to show time, and we've already got a hundred lined up. But the longshoremen and the factory girls are getting off work in five minutes and they are going to be walking by our front door with a week's pay in their pockets. What do you say we give them a little taste?"

"Ready," I say.

"Bianca, my beauty, we'll give them 'The Haymaker's Jig' you've been practicing."

"Got it," she says.

Avrim clips a stray thread from my collar and smooths the front of my vest. I've never had a suit of clothes that somebody hasn't worn before me. It fits perfectly. And it matches the green satin dress with gold trim that he made for Bianca. She's been twirling in it ever since she put it on. Who could blame her? Queen Victoria's own daughters never looked so fine.

We follow Big Al out into the theater and down the middle aisle. Every bit of the place is gleaming, from the velvet seat cushions to the sparkling chandeliers. He puts a penny in the poor box for luck. We step outside and stand under our new sign just unveiled this week. *The Golden Harp*, it says in gold lettering on a green field and then underneath: *Big Al's Family Variety Show*. Dozens of lamps cast a warm glow, and a crisp November wind blows down the street.

"Ladies and gentlemen," Big Al says with a flourish, raising his hat. "Welcome to the Golden Harp!"

There's a scattering of applause and someone from the back shouts "*Erin go bragh!*"

I look up and there is Mr. Ryan the greengrocer, and Matteo the barber and Ivan the butcher waving at me from the crowd. Eliza stands beside them beaming with pride. Her Michael is by her side at last, arm in a sling, but alive.

"We promise you a night of entertainment to warm the hearts of your whole family. Feats of acrobatic skill. Illusions to delight the eye. Music in all the languages you love. And here to share a little preview,

320

the star of our show, our own Danny, the golden boy of Old Ireland! And his little piper girl Bianca!"

We take our spots in front of the box office. Big Al sets down a wooden door for me to dance on. Bianca starts in on "The Haymaker's Jig" on her piccolo. Even before I start I see folks light up when they recognize the tune. I square my shoulders.

"Straight and tall," Packy would say to me.

"Put your heart in it," Ma would say.

I feel a surge of energy as people going by stop to watch.

Bang, shuffle and hop back, bang, shuffle, and hop back.

There's a full row of brass nails in the heel and toe of my shoes, like a proper dancing master. When I jump up to click my heels, they make a crack that you can hear clear down the block. I go on to the second step and change it up with a high kick and a treble rhythm. People start to sway and clap in time. A little girl in the front is dancing along. She doesn't even look Irish to me, but somebody has taught her the very first light jig step I ever learned. *Hop back, two-three-four. Hop front, two-three-four. And skip and skip and one-two-three-four.* She's pretty good for a kid who only comes up to my elbow. I dance up to her and hold out my hand.

"Let's show them what you've got," I say.

She gives me a nervous nod, and I bring her up to the front and wave back the crowd so we have room to dance the lead around together. Bianca goes back to the beginning of the jig. A man who looks like the girl's father takes out a bodhrán and drums a steady tempo. We stand straight and tall. I start to count off the measure and I see this girl square her thin shoulders, point her toe, and lift up her head with pride.

I do the same. And we dance the light jig side by side, here on the crossroads of Ireland and home.

AUTHOR'S NOTE

The Catholic Irish are the indigenous population of Ireland. The English invaded Ireland in 1169, and over many centuries they took Irish property, suppressed the Irish language and culture, enacted laws that made the Irish poor, and created the conditions that made deadly famines a common occurrence. During the Great Hunger of 1845–1852, two million Irish Catholics died while another two million fled to America. A quarter of those died at sea.

The Irish population in America skyrocketed. Before the famine, fewer than ten percent of New Yorkers claimed Irish ancestry. Within a few years, more than twenty-five percent were Irish-born. There was also substantial immigration of German

Catholics in this era. Smaller numbers of Eastern European (including Jewish) and Chinese immigrants came to New York in the mid-1800s, and larger waves of those immigrants would come later.

In America, the Catholic Irish had the vote they'd long sought and been denied in their home country. They used it to organize an effective, but sometimes corrupt, political machine that came to dominate New York politics. This gave them a wildly unfair advantage over black workers, who could not vote. To make matters worse, black workers were denied participation in white unions. When white workers went on strike, employers hired black workers at lower wages to replace them, which led to hard feelings on both sides.

The new Irish immigrants, who had been cruelly oppressed by Protestants in their home country, were deeply distrustful of the American antislavery movement because it was led by Protestants. Nevertheless, when the Civil War began in 1861, the Irish volunteered for military service in high numbers because the signing bonus kept their families from starving—and because they hoped to gain military experience they could use to defeat the British in Ireland. In the ten months between the battles of Antietam and Gettysburg, eighty percent of the Irish Brigade died on the field, disproportionate to every other ethnic brigade in the North. This led to great dismay in the Irish community and ultimately triggered the New York City draft riots of July 11-16, 1863.

The riots began by targeting the draft apparatus itself along with wealthy New Yorkers who had bought their way out of the draft. It expanded into violence against black citizens. In the chaos, many New Yorkers were swept up in the destruction and lost family members, homes, and businesses to fire.

At the start of the war, free black men in the North who volunteered for the army were denied all combat positions, although many did serve in the Navy. Black soldiers began combat operations in the summer of 1863—literally the day after the New York draft riots were put down. They eventually constituted about 10 percent of Union forces and fought with great distinction.

Efforts by the South to stir up more race riots in the North fell flat once black soldiers were serving visibly in combat. The US government also found enough money to pay enlistment bonuses and gave states some flexibility in how they conducted the draft, so that vital services like firefighting could be maintained in local communities.

The Irish continue to immigrate to America, and today 40 million Americans claim Irish heritage. Traditional Irish music and dance, once nearly extinguished, are now a part of the fabric of the American musical and theatrical tradition.

FURTHER READING

Last of the Name depicts the Civil War era through the eyes of an Irish immigrant—one perspective of many. These novels for young readers offer insights into the black experience of the nineteenth century.

Riot by Walter Dean Myers: This screenplay published as a novel follows an interracial family in New York during the 1863 draft riots.

The Madman of Piney Woods by Christopher Paul Curtis: This novel depicts a black community in Canada and its interactions with Irish Immigrants.

The Journey of Little Charlie by Christopher Paul Curtis: In this novel, a slave catcher takes a sharecropper's son north to help him hunt for fugitive slaves.

A Door at the Crossroad and *A Wish After Midnight* by Zetta Elliott: In this time-travel duology, two black teens travel back to Civil War Brooklyn. One finds a free black community there. The other is trapped by blackbirders and taken into slavery in the south. They meet again in the midst of the draft riots.

ACKNOWLEDGMENTS

Irish music and dance is not the culture I grew up with but rather the one my family chose. I am so grateful to the many musicians and dancers who made my family welcome and shared their talents with us. We have spent thousands of hours happily enthralled by jigs and reels and ballads and stories. I have learned from hundreds of singers and musicians, dancers, poets, and storytellers. My particular thanks to Geraldine Murray, Sam and Anne Keator, Elizabeth Nicholson, the Portland Ceili Society, Philip and Pam Boulding, the Raney family, David Ingerson, Laura McLane, and Monica, Brian, Colette and Madelaine Parry. I'm grateful to my agent, Fiona Kenshole, and my critique partners

Michael Gettle-Gilmartin, Cheryl Coupe, Barb Liles and Cliff Lehman. It has been all joy to work with the team at Carolrhoda, including editor Amy Fitzgerald and designer Lindsey Owens. Thank you to Dr. Leslie Harris of Northwestern University, our historical consultant, and to the Library of Congress, The American Irish Historical Society, The Tenement Museum, EPIC the Irish Emigration Museum, The Jeanie Johnson Tall Ship, The Cobh Heritage Center, Trinity College, the Other Voices Music Festival in Dingle, the Dublin song circle An Góilín, and the National Library of Ireland. And most of all thank you to my dance and duet partner Bill for a lifetime of love and support.

TOPICS FOR DISCUSSION

1. As the last surviving boy in his family, what responsibility does Danny have to carry on his family's legacy? How do these expectations affect him?

2. How does Kathleen's Catholic faith shape her decisions? How does the English government's treatment of Irish Catholics affect her views of Protestants in America?

3. Why is music so significant for Irish immigrants like Danny and Kathleen? How does this part of their cultural heritage give them strength? In what ways does it connect Danny to his family?

4. Danny has only ever seen and interacted with white Europeans. How do you think this affects his perceptions of African Americans?

5. What are the similarities and differences between Irish Americans and African Americans? How are their histories different, and how does this affect their futures? Do you think Danny sees the same similarities and differences that you do?

6. Danny overhears an Irish man and woman discussing the war in church. The man thinks that the Irish must prove their worth in the United States by working and fighting harder than the Protestants. The woman thinks that the Irish will all die off if they fight wars for other people. Whom do you agree with? Are Irish immigrants obligated to participate in the war?

7. Danny overhears other Irish immigrants complaining that free black people aren't being drafted into the army. Why do they resent this? What stereotypes play into their opinion of black people?

8. Irish dock workers are angry that black workers broke their strike—agreed to work for lower wages than what the Irish workers demanded. Why do you think the black workers did this? Why do you think the Irish workers don't consider the black workers' motives or needs?

9. Danny has trouble deciding what to believe because of conflicting information in the newspapers he reads. Mr. Treadwell tells him that the newspapers are misleading people and making them prisoners. How does this lack of accurate information make it difficult for the city's different communities to understand each other?

10. The English police force in Ireland was very prejudiced against the Irish when Danny lived there. How does this affect Danny's relationship with the law? What are the similarities and differences between Danny's relationship with the police and African Americans' relationship with the police during the 1800s? How have these relationships changed today?

11. By pretending to be a girl, what does Danny learn about what life is like for girls? How are their lives hard in ways that boys' lives are not? What does Danny miss about living as a boy?

12. Why does the mob start rioting? Do you think they are justified? How do the targets of the violence change over the course of the riots?

13. The carpenters Isaac and Samuel disagree on whether they should join the Union army to

fight the Confederacy. For Isaac and Samuel, what are the similarities and differences between being a slave and being in the army? If you were in their position, what would you do?

14. Who do you think deserves the most blame for the riots: the workers who rioted, the wealthy white people who were exempt from the draft, the newspapers that spread misinformation, the government? What would have to change to prevent this from happening again?

15. What significance does the harp have to Danny and Kathleen? How does it help them start a new life?

16. What do you think will happen to Danny and Kathleen as they grow up? Will Big Al's theater succeed? Will Kathleen become a teacher or a nun, or both? What will Danny's life be like?

ABOUT THE AUTHOR

Rosanne Parry is the award-winning author of several books for children, including *Heart of a Shepherd* and *A Wolf Called Wander*. She can dance a jig and play a hornpipe and is very grateful for the generations of Irish dancers and singers who kept the culture alive in adversity. She lives with her family in an old farmhouse in Portland, Oregon, and works in a treehouse in her backyard.